# LIBERAL IN NATURE

Garrett R. Hall

Copyright 2011 by Garrett R. Hall

All rights reserved. No portion of this book may be reproduced, stored in a retrieval system, or transmitted in any form or by any means – electronic, mechanical, photocopy, recording, scanning, or other – except for brief quotations in critical reviews or articles, without the prior written permission of the author.

LIBERAL IN NATURE

Dedicated to Rachel!

Thanks to God for everything I have! Thanks to my family and friends for their love and support. Special thanks to those who helped with editing: Rachel Hall, Marilynn Monson, Dwight Monson, Molly Monson, Benjamin Monson, Marcus Ryan, Shaun Brown, Keith Kopelson and Nicki Kopelson.

# Table of Contents

TABLE OF CONTENTS.................................................................. 4
CHAPTER 1: THE BEGINNING ..................................................... 6
CHAPTER 2: THE FLIGHT ............................................................ 12
CHAPTER 3: THE ARRIVAL ......................................................... 42
CHAPTER 4: THE TRANSITION ................................................... 58
CHAPTER 5: THE STRUGGLE ...................................................... 65
CHAPTER 6: THE DOE ................................................................ 72
CHAPTER 7: THE ROBIN ............................................................ 82
CHAPTER 8: THE TREES ............................................................. 90
CHAPTER 9: THE APPLES ........................................................... 95
CHAPTER 10: THE BEAR ............................................................ 103
CHAPTER 11: THE WOLF ........................................................... 112
CHAPTER 12: THE BIG BANG ..................................................... 122
CHAPTER 13: THE DUEL ............................................................ 125
CHAPTER 14: THE SALMON ...................................................... 130
CHAPTER 15: THE SQUIRRELS ................................................... 145
CHAPTER 16: THE SOLUTION .................................................... 152
CHAPTER 17: THE WINTER ........................................................ 158
CHAPTER 18: THE SNOW .......................................................... 164
CHAPTER 19: THE RECKONING .................................................. 169
CHAPTER 20: THE TRAP ............................................................ 174
CHAPTER 21: THE CLIMATE ...................................................... 182

CHAPTER 22: THE ATTACK ................................................. 195

CHAPTER 23: THE HERMIT ................................................ 202

CHAPTER 24: THE DEBATE ................................................ 211

CHAPTER 25: THE END ...................................................... 229

CHAPTER 26: THE RETURN ............................................... 233

AFTERWARD ...................................................................... 239

INDEX .................................................................................. 241

# Chapter 1: The Beginning

Andrew sat on a large storage bin as rain gently fell from a sheet of grey clouds and landed on the tin roof of a rundown shack. Four other storage bins and two large coolers lay on the muddy ground around him. A faded sign on the shack read "Arlen's Helicopter Co."

It was 8:30 in the morning and there was no sign of Arlen or his helicopter. Andrew gazed impatiently toward an empty landing pad about thirty feet away. Weeds shot out of the many cracks in the concrete, and Andrew hoped the helicopter was in better shape than everything else in the operation, which looked like it had been completely abandoned.

Doubt crept into Andrew's mind – both about his journey and the transportation – when he heard the faint sound of helicopter rotors. He stood up and wrapped his coat tightly around his body. The sound grew louder and he turned to see a chopper appear over a row of pine trees.

It was a grimy beige (though probably white originally) and overrun with rust, scrapes and dents. The worn down machine looked like it was nearly fifty years old and Andrew was amazed it could get airborne.

As the helicopter descended onto the cracked helipad, it splattered mud and debris onto Andrew and his storage bins. He turned away, cursing under his breath. Wiping mud off his coat and pants, Andrew turned back toward the chopper with an angry scowl.

The blades slowed until they completely stopped. The engine coughed as if it would stop but then kicked in again. A middle-aged man in Army fatigues hopped out and walked toward Andrew as the helicopter engine finally made its last sputter and then died.

"Andrew?" the man asked loudly, as if shouting over a loud noise.

"Yes," Andrew replied, trying to hide his annoyance.

"I'm Arlen. I'll be takin' you up this mornin'. Let me just make a quick adjustment and we'll be on our way. You want to bring your stuff around?"

"Sure," Andrew said, reluctantly eyeing the pilot.

"Can I call you Andy?"

"No. It's Andrew. I go by Andrew."

"Okay, Chief. *Andrew* it is," Arlen said with a kind smile as he turned away.

"I'm a liberal," Andrew announced proudly, but Arlen had already started walking back toward the helicopter and didn't hear him.

Andrew would tell people he was a liberal without any prompting. Before divulging anything about himself to new acquaintances - hometown, background, hobbies, family - he made sure to reveal as soon as possible the fact that he was a liberal. That is how he identified himself on the most fundamental level; When he lay down to sleep at night and all was calm - the moments when people do real soul-searching and take self-inventory - he thought of his liberalism first and everything else secondarily.

Revealing his liberalism at the beginning also helped him to know whether he would befriend the new acquaintance. If the person didn't respond enthusiastically with a "me too!" Andrew knew there wouldn't be much chance of friendship. This technique allowed him to proudly display his liberalism and connect with like-minded enlightened individuals without wasting time on those not intelligent enough to share his views.

Andrew picked up a bin and carried it to the side of the helicopter and then went back for the others.

As he made each trip, he watched Arlen working on the helicopter engine. Arlen appeared to be bending something into place and eventually resorted to pounding away at the uncooperative part with a large wrench.

Andrew wasn't sure what to think about the helicopter and its pilot but he kept hauling his supplies. The enormous coolers, filled with a year's supply of food, were impossible to carry so Andrew had to drag each one through the mud. Before Andrew could back out of his plan, Arlen finished up the adjustment, helped Andrew lift the coolers into the helicopter and they were in their seats.

Andrew was amazed at how fast his life was changing. Twenty-four hours earlier he had awakened from his dream and now here he was on a helicopter headed out into the wilderness. He offered Arlen the map to his destination, but Arlen refused.

"I know where you're goin' based on what you told me on the phone," he said with a smile. "Know these mountains like nothin' else. Could do this blindfolded, but passengers usually don't like it when I do that."

Andrew and Arlen both laughed. Arlen seemed like a decent enough guy, even if he was a simpleton. Andrew always got a kick out of uneducated people because they could be so carefree and happy. It was as if they had more room in their bodies for joy because they had so little knowledge in their brains. Andrew enjoyed being around these blissfully unaware people for limited amounts of time as long as they stuck to telling redneck jokes or tales of their adventures in the backwoods. If they started talking politics or religion, it was over.

Even though he enjoyed Arlen's attempt at humor, Andrew was in a pensive mood. He liked that Arlen had broken it up but he had a lot on his mind and needed some time to think. He was looking forward to soaring over the trees, gathering his thoughts and strengthening his resolve. He hoped that the roar of the helicopter would prevent Arlen from continuing to converse with him.

The engine turned over and the blades started rotating rapidly. As Andrew buckled his seatbelt he couldn't help but notice Glenn Beck's latest book lying on the floor, its pages worn.

"Of course," Andrew thought as he rolled his eyes. "Why wouldn't this ignorant helicopter pilot be a Beck disciple? And why wouldn't I get stuck with him for an hour in a confined space?"

It had been years since he had flown in a helicopter and he was a bit reluctant. The fragile chopper wobbled back and forth a few times and then jerked off the ground, quickly ascending above the tree line. Andrew watched as Arlen's shack grew smaller then disappeared as the helicopter banked toward the mountains.

# Chapter 2: The Flight

Wind poured through a crack in the windshield and Andrew averted his face to avoid the direct impact and to take stock of his traveling companion. Arlen struck Andrew as an older gentleman who strapped a gun to his belt every Sunday to attend church. The camouflage fatigues were a dead giveaway, but the man's simple face and demeanor also revealed his political leaning. Andrew was certain the man had voted against his candidate; he could spot that instantly with most people. His disdain for Arlen necessarily increased.

He looked out the window to distract himself. He wanted to be completely transported to another world. Andrew watched the green foliage pass by as the helicopter soared over mountains and trees at a steady pace. The rush of the wind increased as the helicopter leaned forward and gained momentum.

"What are you doing up in the mountains?" Arlen asked.

Andrew pretended not to hear. He didn't want to have to justify himself to the NRA-supporting wacko. He stared at the mountains silently, hoping Arlen would drop it.

"I say; what are you doing up in the mountains?" the pilot screamed.

"Just trying to get away," Andrew replied with annoyance and contempt.

"I see," said Arlen. "Seen a couple people like you. Go off and live in the forest hopin' to find serenity or trying to dodge the law. Seen it all."

Andrew let out a sarcastic sigh. "Sure, you've seen it all," he thought. "You, the backwoods gun-toting pilot, have seen it all. You have probably lived in your small town your whole life; never been out of the country. You probably didn't even graduate from high school - let alone college. Maybe you got a GED. What could you really have seen? Your simple observations may earn you some recognition down at the local bar, but I don't really care who you are or what you've seen."

Andrew was already anxious to be at his destination. He was tired of society, the pilot, the questions, the election, everything. It was time to start a new life. He didn't know how long he would stay but knew he would stay long enough to avoid the reality of the political situation back home.

He turned his thoughts to his destination, imagining the valley on a warm, sunny day. He thought of hiking to a nearby lake and swimming in the warm water. It was the perfect blend of peace and beauty. He knew political concerns would fade when surrounded by beautiful trees and mountains. He longed for a life in which he didn't have to worry about poll numbers and focus groups. He was tired of spinning things and blaming people for everything that happened. He just wanted to sit peacefully somewhere and reflect on the pure ideals he espoused - his liberalism.

Acres of forested landscape zoomed by below him. Andrew lost his sense of time. He was in a trance as he thought about the journey and what lay ahead. After some time, his mind was rudely pulled back to the confines of the helicopter cabin.

"Did you see the elections last night?" Arlen yelled.

"The Elections!" Andrew thought, as he tried to gain his focus. Over the past 48 hours he had done everything he could to block out the elections, which was not easy considering he was the campaign manager for the most high-profile Senatorial campaign in the cycle. Despite his efforts to gaze out the window and forget, the scene of election night appeared in his mind.

Andrew's worst fears had unfolded throughout the evening. Not only had the liberal incumbent President been defeated in the Presidential election; a "right-wing nut" conservative had defeated him. In addition, the democrats had lost seats in the house and a dozen senate seats, which meant the crazies had significant majorities in both houses *and* a conservative commander in chief.

Andrew had worked furiously over the previous months and years to prevent such an outcome and now he could hardly believe that the ignorance of the people had lead to this disastrous conclusion. He was devastated. He did not know what to do. He was part of a large crowd that had gathered to celebrate the reelection of their progressive leader and to celebrate the recapture of the house. As the votes came in, his colleagues around him became as deflated as he was. Looking around the room he saw shocked faces, as if some tragedy against humanity had just occurred. In Andrew's mind, a human tragedy *had* occurred.

"How could this be?" he thought to himself, but he knew exactly what had happened. He had talked about it with his friends and colleagues in the months leading up to that night. The scare tactics of the right-wing extremists, the fear mongering, the vicious bigotry, the racism, the homophobia and the ignorance of "the people" had triumphed over the hope, change and brilliance they had offered. The people made their choice and they were about to get what they deserved.

They would now have a cold-hearted conservative in charge who had promised to cut down on government spending and entitlement programs, drill in Alaska, repeal health care laws and secure the borders. They had someone who would ruin our restored national image by fighting insensitive and unpopular wars, labeling terrorists and promoting American exceptionalism.

As the reality of the night became apparent, Andrew realized he just couldn't face it. He dropped his campaign posters on the floor, walked by the immaculate buffet table and stumbled toward the door of the luxury hotel banquet hall in a daze. He felt despair. He heard and felt his phone ringing and buzzing but he didn't look at it. He couldn't face anything or anyone. He didn't want to hear condolences and he didn't want to hear jeers. He wanted silence. He wanted stillness. He wanted to hide away somewhere, someplace where no one would find him.

Having escaped the doom of the banquet hall, Andrew found himself in one of the limousines they had rented for the event. He was still so shocked he could hardly move. As the limo drove down the busy street he could see people celebrating and chanting.

"Simpletons," he said. "They don't even know what is good for them. They have no idea what they've done."

Andrew was disgusted by the ignorant people dancing on the sidewalks and celebrating an event that was going to destroy the country. He looked away. He couldn't bear to see it.

"How am I going to take this for four years?" He thought to himself. "How will I live through this? Back to India, perhaps."

Andrew had a difficult time living in the country when a Republican was in the white house. He had fled the country to escape the disastrous consequences of the last Republican Presidency, spending time in Europe, Africa and, eventually, India. He claimed that he wouldn't come back to America until a liberal was in office, but he came back early to help the progressive candidate bring about change. Now that his term was ending, Andrew knew he had to escape.

"I have to leave," he told himself. "I cannot stay."

He made it back to his studio apartment that night. Boxes of campaign bumper stickers, posters, buttons and pennants filled the room. He threw himself onto his bed, having been overcome by fatigue. He had been working day and night in the weeks leading up to the campaign, even knocking on doors in targeted neighborhoods the last few days to encourage people to get out and vote. Weeks of hard work coupled with the emotional ebb and flow of a highly publicized election finally caught up to him and he sank into a deep sleep that would change his life.

His mind jerked back to Arlen's question.

"Nope. I didn't see it," he replied to Arlen.

"Bloodbath, man," said Arlen gleefully. "Dems got creamed. Only a few of them survived. Even *our* Senator got the boot. 'Bout time!"

Andrew could hardly stay in his seat. He wanted to jump up and throw Arlen out of the helicopter. How could he sit there and take political jabs from an uneducated pilot?

"'Bout time for what?" Andrew asked. "'Bout time a right-wing nut jumped in and ruined everything? 'Bout time the country completely went off the deep end? 'Bout time idiots were in charge of the government? What a crock!"

"Hey, just expressing my opinion. Just wanted to see some new blood."

"New blood? So you don't care about good policies; you just want to see some new blood. That new blood is going to take us all down. That new blood is going to ruin everything."

"Well, old guy almost took me down. Carbon taxes, pollution taxes, business taxes; all these taxes hurt a guy like me. Says my helicopter ruins the environment so he punishes me for flyin' it. Funny thing is, he'll take some extra cash to make it all better. If he really cared about the environment and I was hurting it, why not shut me down completely and save the environment? What's more money gonna do? But, I gotta pay it and not ask questions. Here you are, probably thinking my copter is killing the environment too, but here you're riding in it. What am I supposed to do? Had to sell my other copter and let go of my people. Gotta pay the bills. Tough times. Now it's just me runnin' the show here. Just want some new blood, hopefully some new ideas."

"There are no new ideas coming. Those political hacks don't know what they're doing. They are ignorant zealots who have no idea how to transform this nation."

"Nation don't need no transforming. Just need more jobs; need more businesses. I run a business and I don't know what's goin' on. Maybe I'll hire someone and then I get hit with another tax and then I have to fire that person. That don't feel good. Everything's in limbo. Don't know what next month'll hold for me."

"If you understood anything about economics you would know that it's all starting to trickle up. It's coming; or it *was* coming until the conservatives took over. Now I don't know what will happen except that they will cut all the programs we worked hard to start and they will slash government so it won't be able to take care of us."

"Don't need government to take care of me; just

need it to leave me alone. I do fine on my own. I work, pay my taxes, feed my family, go to church, watch a game on Sunday. I'm okay without the government."

"Going to church has really helped you a lot I see," Andrew said sarcastically looking around at the beat up helicopter.

"Done me just fine. I'm a pretty happy guy; got no problem with anyone. Don't have to cut people down to make me feel better 'bout my life. Just live life and treat others good."

"Well," Andrew said.

"Huh?"

"Just live life and treat others *well*," Andrew said. He hated it when people used "good" instead of "well".

"I don't know much," Arlen said. Andrew nodded his head in an exaggerated fashion. "But, I have run this business for thirty years. Been flyin' in these mountains since I was eighteen. My business has survived a lot but it barely survived this last year. It's a scary time. Got a pit in my stomach that won't go away. I worry about my kids and my business all the time. Here I'm flyin' high over the trees in a beautiful place talkin' to you but I'm really thinkin' 'bout making the payment on my house and you haggled me pretty good so I will hardly make money on this flight. Not complainin'; it's just how it is. You ever run a business?"

Andrew hesitated. He knew that he had never run a business and he got defensive every time someone asked him that question. He had taken a few business classes in college so he felt like he understood the concepts better than most of the uneducated people who were running businesses. Besides, he had read so many political books on the economy that he thought he was practically an expert on the subject.

"I've studied business extensively. I know what is involved," Andrew replied authoritatively.

"You ever feel that pit in your stomach? You ever feel the weight of everything coming down on you after you've taken a gigantic risk? You ever go home and look at three kids who have no idea that food might not be on the table the next day and you feel guilty because you know it, but you can't tell them? You ever have to write checks to departments of government you've never even heard of? Meanwhile, your wife is out at garage sales trying to buy cheap clothes for the kids cause there's no money left and those cute buggers are growin' like weeds?"

Arlen paused. He was getting choked up so he looked out his window. He wiped his cheeks with his oily gloves.

"I know there's people who got it worse than me. We try to give to the church and help those folks. I volunteer my copter when someone goes missin'. We make meals for folks who got nothin'. We try to do our part to help the needy. But, just seems that we can handle that and don't need the government babysittin' and takin' our money to take care of people who aren't doin' a lick of work tryin' to get into a better situation. Those people only see a bit of that money anyway seeing how the government wastes so much of it. I just think things need to change. We're not going to make it the way we're going. Got that pit in my stomach all the time. Won't go away. Wake up in the middle of the night worrying. Can't eat as much. Can't relax and take my mind off of it. It's always there."

Andrew was fuming. He couldn't believe what this guy was saying. He clearly had bought into the conservative, tea party crap and didn't have the education to see through to reality.

"That's a nice story," Andrew started sarcastically. "But, I don't think you really understand what the government does. Those people who benefit from the government would have nothing without us. They have a right to have the things that others have and we have an obligation and duty to give it to them. It's not fair for some to suffer and experience poverty while a few of us have it all. They deserve some of that. They deserve to live the American dream just like the rest of us. If Tea-partiers got their way, those people would all die of starvation and pneumonia while everyone else – all the good Christians – stand aside and watch. It is such hypocrisy. It is so wacko I can't even begin to describe it."

"I think you misunderstood me. I'm not saying I don't care about those people. In fact, I do care a lot and that is why I think they should have a chance to stand on their own. See if they can make the American dream happen for themselves. American dream don't guarantee anything except that you have freedom to make something happen. It's got nothin' to do with money or status. It's about freedom and opportunity. Poor man can still live the American dream, while a rich man can miss it. I had nothin' growing up. Barely finished high school. Had nothin' lined up; took a job fixin' engines. That moved into working on helicopters. Did that for years. Saved up some money and bought this helicopter from a fella' who couldn't get it to run. I worked on it and fixed it and then got my pilot's license and became a pilot. Business has been up and down but it's *my* business and I can make of it what I want. Maybe not *your* American dream, but it's mine and I'm happy with it."

"That's great but you got that chance. Some people don't have that chance. They are stuck and can't get out of their situation. That is where the government helps them. What would they do without it?"

"Maybe somethin'. Maybe nothin'. Who knows? But what do they do with it? Most them folks don't go nowhere cause no one gives 'em a kick in the butt. When I was eighteen my dad told me to get out and find a job so I did. My friend's dad didn't tell him nothin'; just let him sleep in the basement, gave him food and stuff. He's still there. Never forced to go out and get somethin'. Shame too. He was a smart kid; coulda' been somethin' great if he'd been pushed out the house. Instead he goes from job to job not caring about anything. Lives off the government. Never been pushed; never felt that pit in his stomach."

"Again, great story but not really reality. Studies have shown that government programs do help people improve their situations."

Andrew stopped himself. He was getting into too much detail and he was letting Arlen control the conversation. He had wanted to just finish the conversation and move on to his adventure in the wilderness but he couldn't let it go. He had to put Arlen in his place. Andrew instinctively resorted to his campaign rhetoric.

"If you think the tea-partiers know what they're doing, then you're either ignorant or dishonest. All of those candidates are wackos. They have no experience, they have radical ideas and they are incredibly stupid. Not to mention the fact that they are bigots, homophobes and racists. The fact that they

## LIBERAL IN NATURE

won any election from city council to the Presidency just validates the ignorance of the American public. It just shows the sad state of affairs of those who vote. They are so easily swayed by promises to cut spending, reduce the deficit and shrink government. They don't understand that, first, it will never happen. Second, if it did happen, the country would fall apart. People need the government. The government creates jobs and opportunities. The government runs important programs, protects citizens, regulates industries, protects the environment, and helps people who cannot help themselves.

Your tea party candidates are just ignorant Joes who want to play dress-up politician but they don't know how things really work. They have no idea how to run a country because they're idiots and they don't have the intellectual qualifications to be in politics. And here you are complaining about government when you have probably never even been to Washington D.C. You're a simple pilot who flies up and down and around the mountains. What kind of experience do you have? Where have you been and what have you done? People like you voted out the only chance we've got and you probably couldn't even name the Vice President. People like you chose for everyone else and you have never even been to a college class. What do you know about the economy? You get your information from Fox News or from your Pastor."

Having dealt Arlen a heavy blow, Andrew leaned back and stretched his legs.

"I only know what I've experienced. I only know the fear of taking a big risk and having to make things happen each day. Those politicians, they get paid regardless of what they do. Most of 'em never run a business. Most never got those letters in the mail from the Department of Revenue or Labor and Industries or Treasury. I don't think they get it. Oh well. What can I really do about it? I'm just one person. Cast my vote and then hope someone gets it right."

"You can get educated and vote for the right person, first of all. Second, you can pay your taxes with pride and patriotism, knowing that you are supporting the country. If you do it grudgingly as you apparently do, it is as if you didn't do it," Andrew knew he had heard something like that before, but couldn't remember where it came from.

"I don't give to the church grudgingly. Don't help people grudgingly. Don't give meals or service to people grudgingly. I have a choice in doing those things. No one is forcing me so I get to choose and believe, which makes me a better person. It is true charity and love. Got no choice in paying the government. Don't make me a better person. Don't help me overcome selfishness. It's just pay or get in big trouble."

"You are helping the country. It is a patriotic

# LIBERAL IN NATURE

thing to do. Take pride in it and enjoy that feeling of knowing that you are helping people."

"Helping or enabling?" Arlen questioned as he banked the helicopter hard to the right.

"Enabling?" Andrew was furious at this point. He couldn't believe this man was so ignorant and ungrateful for everything Andrew and his colleagues had done to help his state and the country. He was amazed that people like this pilot were allowed to vote. He thought they should come up with a simple test to determine voter eligibility. Prerequisite questions would include: Do you believe the fact that people and corporations are causing climate change? Do you believe that it is the Government's job to take care of its people? Do you believe that there should be more equality in wages and overall wealth? If anyone answered "no" to any of the questions, they should be prevented from voting.

"Sometimes you have to –"

Andrew was interrupted by something he saw below him. He couldn't believe it but as the helicopter banked to the right he was looking down on his destination. It looked so beautiful and peaceful. Arlen made a wide circle around the whole valley and Andrew could see everything: the river, lake, meadow and mountains. It was just as he had seen in his dream.

The morning after the election, Andrew had

awakened feeling much better. His sleep had produced the most amazing dreams he had ever experienced. Waking up from such vivid and clear dreams was like a new birth for him, though he didn't know why yet. He was waking up but he wanted to go back into his dreams. He wanted to escape the world and live in the blissful peace he had experienced all night, but he also wanted to bring the blissful peace of his dreams into the world. He sat up and looked around his room.

It had taken him a minute to figure out where he was, which was not uncommon with all of the traveling he did and all the hotels in which he stayed. He looked around, trying to make sense out of his current surroundings. Once he saw the campaign signs piled up he remembered the night before - the election and the end of life as he knew it. The pain started to creep back into his mind as he remembered watching the election results, but it was halted by something; the dream.

Sitting up quickly, the memory came to his mind, as did the peaceful feelings he felt during the dream. His mind scrambled to recall everything about the dream. He visualized the celestial valley, animals, greenery, mountains, harmony and beauty.

He kept a notebook by his bed to write thoughts that came to him during the night; campaign strategies, things he had to do, deep thoughts, etc. He grabbed the notebook and starting writing about the details he recalled from his dream.

He found himself back in the luxury banquet room awaiting the election results. The excitement and euphoria still permeated the crowd as they waited for the results and hoped for an all-out victory for the democrats. Just before the first disappointing results came back, Andrew was whisked away by some force that carried him through the walls and ceilings of the hotel and out into the dark of night. He felt no fear. The force was peaceful and comforting. It suddenly carried him at high speeds to a place far away. After traveling for only a few moments he found himself in a beautiful mountainous valley on a warm, sunny day.

The warmth of the sun seemed to soak into his body and warm his very soul. He stretched out his arms and looked to the sky. Then he looked around him. He was in a luscious valley, which felt like home. He stood in a field of green grass. Evergreen trees jutted up on the perimeter of the field interspersed with aspens and shrubbery. A river snaked along the west side of the valley then emptied into a small lake only a few hundred yards from where he stood. The lake reflected the trees and mountains to the west. At the southern tip of the lake was a large and vast beaver dam and just below it a small stream flowing south. Deer drank from the stream, squirrels scampered to and from trees, a bear splashed in the river and fish jumped out of the lake and dived back into it. It was the most beautiful valley he had ever seen.

As he watched, he noticed that the animals lived and moved in harmony and peace. All the animals looked healthy and happy. The bear was swimming joyfully in the river while salmon swam right next to it. The squirrels gathered nuts for each other and shared everything they had. The hawk would swoop down into the field and fly right over the field mouse but would not snatch it. The trees grew spontaneously and all the plant life looked healthy and lush.

Andrew was astonished. The valley offered such a contrast to what he knew in society. The harmony he saw brought such peace and pure happiness to his heart that he felt like leaping up and down and screaming for joy. His pain and anguish were replaced with such exhilaration that he wanted to leave everything and go to this place. He almost felt compelled to go there, as if it was his duty.

Just as he was starting to settle down and become a part of the beautiful valley, he was whisked away by the same force that brought him there and was transported almost instantly back into the luxurious banquet hall. As soon as his feet touched down, the dream had ended.

Sitting on the edge of his bed and writing notes to retrieve the vibrant images, Andrew had drawn a map of the valley. Something clicked in his mind and he realized that he recognized the valley. He had hiked through it on a long backpacking trek many years earlier, though he hadn't noticed everything from his dream at that time. He hadn't been back because the EPA had long since closed the trails leading to the valley in order to protect an endangered vermin.

"I've been there," Andrew said. "But I was much more immature then and I did not understand things the way I do now."

Looking at the map on the paper he knew what he would do. He couldn't stand to live through another four years of a Republican president - a conservative, much less. He needed an escape. He had to go *somewhere*, but he was tired of the inconveniences of living overseas and didn't want to go back to Canada. He had to get away and this dream was the answer. He would go into the wilderness and live life in nature with the animals, plants and rocks. This was the solution he needed.

A new energy flowed through him as he developed a plan. He jumped up and started grabbing clothes and stuffing them into a nearby duffel bag. He grabbed his notebook again and started listing items that he would need for his journey.

"My journey?" He questioned himself. "No. My exodus. I will leave the slavery of conservatism and republicanism and will find my promised land. The valley is my promised land. I can't stay here and watch this new president destroy *my* country."

His thoughts raced as he contemplated staying in society and having to endure the destruction of the welfare program and all else that he and other liberals had worked so hard to accomplish. He couldn't stand the thought.

His mind wandered back to previous Republican Presidencies and the daily incompetence they had displayed. He had been forced to migrate to other countries. When people would ask him where he was from, he would tell them he was Canadian. He did not want anything to do with the United States and the President – a man he thought should be punished by a war tribunal and sentenced to death. This new President might actually be worse. He felt that his country was in serious danger.

Andrew stopped planning and sat down again on his bed.

"Could this be real?" he thought. "Am I really going to leave everything behind to live in a valley that might not exist the way I imagine it? Can I really do that based on a dream alone? What is my basis for doing this? Am I really thinking reasonably? Is this rational?"

Questions flooded his mind as he contemplated this new plan.

"This seems like something my family members

would do. They would claim to have some sort of divine revelation that commanded them to go into the wilderness. For years their silly "promptings" had led their lives instead of science and reason. His parents, and later his siblings, claimed feelings that cannot be proved and based those feelings on their belief in a God whose existence they could not prove. They put their faith in fleeting emotions and blindly follow a religious organization that tells them what to do with their time and money. They have thrown thousands of dollars down the drain because of that faith. They claim that God created the earth and that he lives somewhere in heaven and that someday he will return to the earth and yet they don't believe in the big bang, which is provable by science."

Andrew's thoughts turned to the whims of his family's religion. They always talked about "feelings" and "impressions" but could never really back it up with anything substantive. He hated it. They talked about faith as if it was the only way to live and that, if you didn't have faith, you were somehow missing out on some potential. He knew that religion was the cause of most of society's problems and was responsible for war and hate. He tried to enlighten his family as to this fact every opportunity he got, but they never comprehended the truth.

"How is my dream any different?" He thought. "What is it based on? A dream? Where do dreams come from?"

Andrew remembered a grant he had worked on while in D.C. that gave 14.5 million dollars to researchers in order to determine where dreams originated and why people have them. He remembered that the results of the study showed that dreams come from our own experiences as processed by our brains and sent to the subconscious portions of our minds, which are the parts of our anatomy that produce dreams. The study, while inconclusive, stated that with additional funding the group would be able to prove that dreams have scientific grounding and could be explained using purely scientific means.

"My dream did take place in nature, which is science," Andrew reasoned. "The dream dealt with zoology, geology, geography, botany, entomology, hydrology, meteorology and other ologies. It was all about being in nature and studying and exploring science. There is no religious purpose involved. There is no promise of spiritual enlightenment. The purpose of the dream was not to enslave myself or others as religion does. So my purpose is one of science and not religion. The feelings I had were actually factual triggers – memories – since I have been to this place before. I know it exists. These triggers weren't really feelings at all, but were scientific messages instead. It was the anatomical pieces of my brain sending electronic impulses regarding messages of science and reason."

Since terms like "exodus" and "journey" had religious overtones, he decided to title his endeavor an "expedition". He thought it sounded more scientific and adventurous than some journey to a make-believe promised land or a forty-year exodus in the desert. Besides, the car he drove was an "Expedition" so he thought it was a good title for this trip.

As he contemplated his new scientific expedition his energy was renewed. He continued his preparation while also planning in his head. His years of experience in campaigning had fine-tuned his ability to work furiously on something while planning and strategizing his next step.

Andrew was no stranger to the outdoors. Since he was a small boy, his dad had taken him and his brothers camping, fishing and hunting at least once every two months. They had been all over the state where he grew up. They had even taken annual trips to Canada and Alaska searching for beautiful locations, big fish and trophy bucks. And though he had denounced his past as a hunter, he hadn't lost the survival skills his dad had taught him.

His dad had spent summers commercial fishing in Alaska, building trails and fences in mountainous regions in the western United States and camping in snow, rain, heat and nearly every weather condition imaginable. He was an expert survivor, both in the wilderness and in society and he had always tried to teach those skills to his children.

Once while on a backpacking trip they had lost their way and been bludgeoned by a ferocious rain and wind storm for three days straight. They managed to build shelters, find food, stay warm and relatively dry. They even succeeded in enjoying themselves by playing cards and talking about sports.

Andrew's dad felt it was important to bequeath his survival knowledge to his children so they could enjoy the outdoors as he always had and so they could survive in the brutal world of man. He used to say as they hiked, "surviving out here is nothing compared to surviving in society." He would also say, "if anything ever happened to my family, I would come out here and live off the land."

Andrew always understood what his dad meant about surviving in society, though, instead of running from it he decided to devote his life to making survival more accessible for people. As he studied in College he questioned why it was so difficult for people to survive. "They shouldn't have to struggle for the necessities of life", he thought. He wanted to take away the struggle. He felt that he owed it to people to help them survive.

As a new president had now been elected on the promise that he would cut spending and entitlement programs, Andrew realized that the balance was

## LIBERAL IN NATURE

quickly shifting and it would once again be easier to survive in nature than in society. Now Andrew would get the experience of surviving in the wilderness.

Suddenly he was jerked back to reality as the helicopter descended. Andrew's eye caught sight of four deer spring away into the woods just as he'd seen in his dream. He could see birds flying from tree to tree and squirrels bounding all over. He was so amazed at the view he had that he asked Arlen to circle a few more times. Andrew quickly got his notebook out and drew a rough map of the valley. He wanted to take advantage of the vantage point so he could remember where various points of interest were.

When he finished, he motioned for Arlen to put the helicopter down. Arlen flew over the lake and hovered for a moment over a bare, flat area just east of the lake. The helicopter started on its final descent. Andrew was full of excitement and awe as he was lowered to the ground. He anticipated all of the animals stopping what they were doing to watch him descend out of the sky.

Andrew felt like a God coming down to mingle in the affairs of man, except that he would be mingling in the affairs of animals and plants and *he* actually existed.

Andrew wished the animals could sense the important person he was so as to gain their trust right away. He wished particularly they could know how much he had already done to save them and their environment. He did not typically like the word "savior", but he thought that it actually fit in this case. He had really worked hard and pushed to help these animals have a place to live, clean water to drink and fresh air to breathe. They owed so much of what they had to him.

Of course, they couldn't possibly know this but Andrew hoped that they might sense it. He wanted to befriend them. He knew that without any other people there, he would need to have some friends.

The helicopter had nearly touched the ground when he noticed a few animals looking at him. Two squirrels stood on their heals watching him touch down. The birds seemed to have retreated to their nests. The deer had leaped away but he guessed they were probably watching him from their hiding places. It seemed to Andrew that the whole valley had stopped to welcome him. The movement he had seen from above had all but ceased and all eyes were on him as he touched down onto the ground.

The helicopter blade slowed and Arlen motioned that Andrew could get out. He stepped onto the soft ground and stood motionless for a minute to gaze at his new surroundings. He couldn't believe he could now call the valley "home". Even standing next to the helicopter, the air was crisp and pure. He inhaled deeply trying to take in as much of the valley as he could. He then moved out from underneath the helicopter blade and planted his feet firmly into the soft soil.

Arlen, meanwhile, was unloading all of Andrew's supplies and placing them at the base of a nearby tree. Andrew could feel the tenderness of the earth under his feet as his new hiking boots sunk ever so slightly into the earth. He was becoming part of nature. The temperature was cool but it was a comfortable coolness. Fall was in the air. Andrew buttoned up his coat as he continued gazing out into the beautiful wilderness.

Arlen whistled to Andrew and broke him out of his spell. He had unloaded all of Andrew's supplies and was ready to take off. Andrew reluctantly shook Arlen's outstretched hand.

"No hard feelings, right brother?" Arlen said. "I didn't mean to complain and criticize anyone. I'm sure they're doing their best."

"They are," Andrew replied confidently. "I argue politics for a living so I'm sorry I had to do that to you. Thanks for the lift. Good luck flying home."

"Thanks. You want me to check on you if I'm in the area? Bring you some supplies?"

"Maybe in the spring," Andrew said. "We'll see."

"Alright. Good luck up here. Stay warm."

With that Arlen walked to his door and hopped

into the helicopter. The blades started spinning faster and the hum of the engine grew louder. Andrew watched as the helicopter rose above him sending leaves, dirt and debris in all directions. He partially shielded his face with his hands as he watched the copter rise high into the air and fly west, leaving a trail of smoke behind.

"Maybe we *should* shut him down completely," Andrew said as he brushed dirt off of his coat and pants for the second time. "Look what he did to my valley."

Andrew shook his head as he looked at the harm and disruption Arlen had caused to the valley.

"And what is the deal with running into so many conservative crazies all of the sudden," Andrew wondered, as his mind recalled the last twenty-four hours he had spent prepping for his expedition. "I have gone weeks and months without having to deal with these freaks and now it's like they are everywhere. At least I won't run into any up here."

Andrew thought of Arlen as he watched the copter disappear over the mountains to the west. He pitied him. Arlen seemed like a decent guy and Andrew actually liked him, but his policies and ideas were so crazy Andrew just couldn't respect him. It wasn't his fault the guy never got an education and learned how things should work. Andrew didn't feel bad about destroying him in the argument and making him look ridiculous, but he wished that politics had never come up.

"Maybe someday he will figure it out," Andrew thought to himself, though he did not really think it very likely.

# Chapter 3: The Arrival

Andrew immediately got to work setting up camp. He wanted to explore the valley extensively but also knew that establishing a camp was first priority. Finding flat ground under a few trees, he set up his tent. He moved his storage bins close to his ten-man tent, which had three separate rooms. He designated the rooms; bedroom; pantry/kitchen; and office.

Knowing it was important for him to stay busy and organized, Andrew started creating jobs as he tried to establish a routine. The office contained paperwork and scientific instruments that he intended to use to measure temperatures and conduct other scientific studies. The pantry contained two large coolers, one of which he would use as a table, along with three camping chairs so he could sit and enjoy meals. The bedroom contained his sleeping bag, air mattress, sleeping pad and three bins of clothing labeled: "winter", "summer" and "spring/fall".

Exerting concentrated effort for hours, everything inside the tent was finally in order.

"Not a bad little home," he thought, admiring his new abode.

Anxious to explore and get in touch with his surroundings, Andrew decided to cover a square mile before the sun went down. He grabbed his rifle and a box of ammunition out of one of the bins.

Andrew hated guns, which he blamed for the problems of violence in the country. He and his political allies worked for years to pass sweeping legislation banning handguns, but it was always delayed. Polls showed the majority of people in his state opposed the ban, but Andrew believed it would benefit the state in ways the people did not understand.

They pushed it forward and it became a hotly debated issue full of emotion and opinion. The effort was not successful so they shelved it until the people could be educated or until they could attach it to some other bill and get it passed quickly. They were, however, successful in passing legislation requiring background checks and waiting periods.

"It's a good start," Andrew always said about the bill, even though he was disappointed they weren't able to pass the full version.

As he now loaded his rifle, he thought of the

conservative who sold it to him the day before. Buying a gun was not something he ever thought he would do. He had reluctantly made the purchase because he knew he would need it for his safety.

Andrew had entered the gun store cautiously. He felt like he was entering enemy territory and all the enemies were armed with weapons.

"If my friends saw me right now, they'd kill me," he thought.

As he entered the store, a man behind the counter greeted him and asked if he could help. Andrew decided to accept his help so he could get out of there as fast as possible.

"Do you have a handgun that will take down a bear?" he asked.

The man smiled and motioned for Andrew to walk to the far end of the counter.

"This here is a 44 magnum. Take this, put these bullets in it and you'll take down a bear." The man threw down a box of shells as he spoke. "You ought to be careful hunting bear with a handgun."

"Oh, I'm not hunting them," Andrew replied. "I just want to be sure I can stop one if it's hunting *me*," he said.

The man laughed. "That's mighty wise of you. Where you headed?"

Andrew paused momentarily. He hadn't really

told anyone his plans and he became worried about what the man might say to him. Andrew thought the guy might try to tell him he couldn't do it or that he was crazy.

"I am going to live in the wilderness for a while. I'm trying to get away."

The man looked Andrew over and said, "Every man has thought of doing that at some point in his life; including me. I envy you."

"Thanks," Andrew said, surprised at the man's answer. He had expected ridicule and mocking. He was impressed by the man's ability to relate to him, especially since he didn't expect such understanding from his own friends. They would accuse him of going redneck or deserting the country when it needed him most.

"Shoot. If you're going all Jeremiah Johnson, let me show you some things," the man said with growing excitement.

The man took Andrew to another part of the store and began showing him a variety of survival supplies. He told Andrew about when he had lived in the wilderness for six months and the lessons he had learned. Andrew was amazed at the man's knowledge and experience. He ended up with a 44 magnum and twenty boxes of ammunition, a rifle with twenty boxes of ammunition and additional survival supplies, including a new hunting knife.

As he walked to the front of the store, Andrew felt like he would be prepared for anything, though he didn't think he would ever even shoot the guns. He was excited about the items he was purchasing and had actually enjoyed conversing with the gun store guy. He had a great time listening to the man's stories and they laughed as they gathered the supplies. Andrew was grateful for the help.

"Good luck up there. I hope you find everything you're looking for. Sometimes a man's got to get away and find out what he's made of. You will do great!" The man was very encouraging and Andrew felt like it was authentic. He was glad that he came in the store and met the guy. He wished that he had more friends like him and he realized that the guy reminded him of his father.

"Thanks for all your help," Andrew said as he handed the guy his credit card.

"No worries, man. That's what I'm here for," the man said as he took Andrew's credit card. "I will just need you to fill out some paperwork for the handgun. Then, we'll do a background check and you can pick it up in five days."

"What?" Andrew said.

"A background check," the man said. "Senator's orders. Wasn't always like that. Used to be you could walk outta here with a forty-four with no questions asked. Now, we've got to do all kinds of paperwork for background checks and waiting periods. Huge burden, if you ask me. It's slowed sales a lot and pissed off customers but the government says I need to do it. They say it prevents crimes of passion. Don't know about that, but I do know that I have to do it."

Andrew was torn. He had fully supported the five-day waiting period and would have preferred more time. It was a great idea, but now that he had to wait, it was frustrating. When he was pushing the legislation he never considered that it might affect him someday. He knew he wasn't a threat to anyone; he wasn't going to shoot anyone in the heat of passion. While he supported the law, he knew that it was meant for other people - not him.

"Any way around that?" Andrew asked.

"'Fraid not," the man said. "They really keep tabs on that kind of stuff. I wish I could help you out."

"I'm leaving tomorrow. I can't go without a handgun but I can't wait five days. I need it *now*!"

"Listen, man. If it were up to me, I would do it in a heartbeat but my hands are tied. I cannot break the law or they will shut me down. It's kind of a silly law but I still have to comply."

"But it doesn't apply to me," Andrew said, increasingly frustrated. "It was meant for everyone else."

"Everybody says that."

"Alright," Andrew said, showing his extreme

annoyance. "I will take the rifle and all the other stuff and leave the handgun."

As the man swiped his card, Andrew looked up at the wall behind the man's head. There were pictures of hunters standing over their kills, newspaper cutouts and bumper stickers. Right in the middle of it all was a picture of the Senator for whom Andrew had worked so many years. Above his head it read "Wanted" and below it, "For infringing our second amendment rights". This infuriated Andrew. He had liked this guy a lot, but he couldn't handle such ignorance.

The man handed the credit card slip to Andrew. As he signed his name, he said, "You know the second amendment does not apply to handguns."

"What?"

"I was just reading your 'wanted' poster and thought you should know that the second amendment doesn't apply to handguns."

"Supreme Court disagrees with you."

"Well I disagree with the Supreme Court because it's wrong. It's a conservative court and doesn't understand the Constitution. Bunch of hateful, homophobic, idiot judges who don't know anything about what is good for the country."

"I hadn't pegged you as a left-winger. Usually I can spot you hypocrites as soon as you walk through the door. So, you know more about the Constitution than the Supreme Court Justices?"

"I know more about the Constitution than at least *five* of the Justices! They don't think about public policy enough. They won't see the Constitution as a living document that needs to evolve with the times. They have no idea –"

"Get out of my store!" the man said abruptly, interrupting Andrew. "Take your factless, whiny, I-know-better-than-everyone-else-because-I-took-a-college-class attitude and go on up to the mountains. It will do you some good; knock some sense into you! I hope it helps you to see reality, boy. Maybe you'll see that you don't know anything about anything just like the rest of us. Might give you some humility. Go on!"

Andrew was shocked. No one had ever spoken to him like that about his political opinions. He was usually able to argue enough to get people to give up and concede. He could normally argue in circles until he confused the person enough to stop arguing. He thought about just leaving, but he had to get a couple shots in on his way out.

"That was an intelligent response. I am astounded by your eloquence and rhetorical abilities. You really are gifted."

"I know what you're doing and you can just stop right now. Don't make this about me. What do you want from me? I'm a guy in a gun shop. But, that doesn't make my arguments invalid. Attacking me won't get you anywhere, except maybe your face bashed in a little. I have faced off against enough of you libtards to know what you're going to do. So, rather than go through the whole charade, just walk away and tell yourself that I'm an ignorant fool who doesn't know anything. Make yourself feel better and protect your precious opinions by making it all about me. Heaven forbid you should actually listen to something someone has to say. It might dash all your liberal dreams if you stop to consider another viewpoint. So, just walk away and convince yourself that all your opinions are fact and anyone who disagrees with you is an idiot."

Andrew wasn't sure what to do. This man, while he was clearly a moron, seemed to be more informed than most conservatives. He could articulate and he could make the weak conservative arguments in an aggressive and belligerent manner. Andrew regrouped and went in for the kill.

The man looked at Andrew and then picked up a red book and put it up to his face in an exaggerated fashion suggesting the conversation was over. Instead of looking at the man's face, Andrew was instead looking at a picture of a man in a brown hat holding a sign that read "Stopping Obama's Attack on Our Borders, Economy, and Security." Andrew had no idea how to respond to the man's psychotic rant or his choice of literature so he grabbed his stuff and walked to the door. As he was pushing the door open with his back, he looked at the man and said, "You *are* an idiot! That's a fact."

Andrew left the store extremely annoyed. He wished the guy had never said anything political. He liked him and preferred not knowing how misinformed he was. Any respect he had for him was now gone.

By the time he had loaded his car and started to drive away, he was over it. He had battled uninformed right-wingers so many times that he had an uncanny knack for not dwelling on the conversations. He believed the reason people stew over heated conversations is because as they replay the argument in their minds they are concerned that either they didn't perform well, or the other person could have been completely or partially right.

Andrew, therefore, never questioned his own ability – he considered himself to be undefeatable in political arguments – and he never entertained the idea that the other person may have been even partially correct. This made it very easy to move on and not let the conversation bother him.

The last bullet clicked into place. Andrew stood up and tried to bring his mind back to the present as he looked over the valley.

"What a moron that guy was," he said as he slung the rifle over his shoulder. "I'm so glad to be free of idiots out here."

He started his exploration by walking along the banks of the river that ran close to his camp. The river was about twenty yards across and about three or four feet deep in the middle. It narrowed in parts and got deeper and faster. In other spots, it was slow and wide. There were a few deep pools, which Andrew noted would be good for fishing. As he walked along the river he noticed birds flying around anxiously and squirrels scurrying up and down trees.

Andrew worried that the animals feared him. They acted like he was a danger to them. He knew it would take time to convince them that he was a protector but he wanted to establish his role as soon as possible. Walking slowly and deliberately, he tried to take in all of the beauty of the world around him while also trying to fit in. He came upon a deep pool in the river where a saw a beaver gliding back and forth.

The beaver had constructed an impressive dam and was basking in the slow-moving water. Andrew watched for a few minutes and noticed three other smaller beavers in the pool.

"A cute little beaver family," he said to himself.

He tried to imagine how it would feel to be a beaver. He knew he would have to understand the animals if he were ever going to earn their trust. He watched as the beaver glided effortlessly through the clear water.

"What a beautiful home. The location is pretty dam good," he said smiling, as he thought of his dad and his love for puns.

Looking at the neatly constructed dam, he admired the beavers' craftsmanship. He imagined that it must have taken it weeks to gather the sticks and place them perfectly. All the hard work seemed to have paid off now that the beaver family was able to enjoy the deep pool.

As Andrew looked closer he noticed something that didn't look right. In the middle of the beaver's dam was a bright blue object. He couldn't tell what it was but he knew it was not natural and, therefore, had no business being in a place like this. Andrew was furious.

"How did that get here? Who would have come all the way up here?"

He walked to the edge of the river to get a better look at the object. It was a blue tarp. Andrew couldn't believe someone had allowed this foreign object to pollute the clear, natural river. He was embarrassed by the human race and saw this as an opportunity to show the beaver and all animals that he was not like other humans. He figured any previous visitors to the valley must have been redneck hunters who would not have left a favorable impression, but apparently left a tarp. That being the case, he could understand the animals' reluctance to get close to him. Andrew shared that same reluctance when it came to hunters and conservatives.

"To think that I might be lumped in with *them*," he thought with a shudder.

Andrew wanted to show the animals that he was different and this was his chance. He decided that if he were a beaver he wouldn't want to swim around in this deep pool with an ugly blue eye sore.

"Sorry beavers!" he yelled. "Some people messed up your home because they were arrogant and careless. I'm sorry about them. They think they rule the world. Don't worry, though, I am going to fix this."

The tarp was about fifteen feet from the bank, and Andrew thought he could reach it by crawling carefully on top of the dam. The beaver and her young ones had stopped swimming and were floating motionless on the other side of the river. Their tiny black eyes were focused squarely on Andrew. He was glad the beavers were watching so they would know that Andrew was the one who had removed the ugly object from their home.

Stepping onto the dam, he carefully scaled it using his hands in front. His weight made the sticks sink a few inches, soaking his shoes. Annoyed, because he hated getting his shoes wet, Andrew felt it was a small concession to gain the beavers' trust. He made it to the middle of the dam and hunched above the tarp. He glanced up to make sure the beavers were still watching him. They hadn't taken their beady eyes off him.

"Don't worry," he called to them. "I'm going to fix everything!"

Stretching lower to the water, he reached his hand toward the tarp, grabbed an edge and pulled it toward him. At first it came easily but then something caught. Thinking it was lodged on a stick, he yanked it with all his strength. The sticks underneath him started to move. He couldn't figure out what was happening but it felt like he was getting pulled downstream.

Acting quickly, he pulled on the tarp again as he made his way back to the shore. This time the tarp came dislodged and Andrew hurriedly scaled the dam as it was suddenly collapsing under him. He turned to see water rushing through the middle of the dam where the tarp had been, taking sticks, branches and all the beavers' hard work with it.

Within a few seconds the entire dam had been washed downstream and the deep pool had disappeared. There was no sign of any of the beavers. Andrew was in shock, standing silently on the bank with soggy feet.

He looked at what used to be a beaver dam and shook his head.

"If those redneck hunters hadn't littered the valley with their tarp -" he said without finishing the thought.

He hurried back to camp and threw the tarp on the ground in exasperation.

"What a dam disaster, but at least the beavers won't have to look at that ugly tarp anymore," he thought to himself.

Andrew entered his tent and fell on his bed. He had only rested for a few minutes when he heard raindrops on top of the tent. The drops started out softly and infrequently but soon were beating down more rapidly. He looked outside and the ground was already wet. He was glad that all of his supplies were in plastic bins so the water wouldn't damage anything, though he was disappointed that he couldn't organize the camp more.

The evening was setting in. As Andrew relaxed on the bed he realized how fatigued he was. All of the planning, arranging, shopping, flying, and setting up had taken a toll. He closed his eyes and began to mumble a song.

"Come gather round people;
Wherever you roam;
And admit that the waters around you have grown;
And accept it that soon you'll be drenched to the bone;

If your time to you is worth saving;
Then you better start swimming or you'll sink like a stone;
Oh the times, they are a-changin."

With that, Andrew fell into a deep sleep and didn't awake until sunrise.

# Chapter 4: The Transition

In the morning, Andrew could hear rain still beating against his tent. His mind hadn't made the transition and thoughts of his old life still lingered. Twenty-four hours before, he had taken a taxi to Arlen's Helicopter Co and only forty-eight hours had passed since his dream.

He still couldn't believe how fast it had all happened. That was how Andrew did things, though. Once he made up his mind to do something, he did it right away. Once he came up with a plan or idea, he implemented it immediately and pushed it forward with all his strength and energy. He had only required one day to prepare for his expedition.

Andrew already had the regular camping equipment but he had to buy several other items besides his gun. Because of the volume of items he needed – camping supplies, non-perishable foods, seeds, clothes – he wanted to go to discount stores. However, he did not want to run all over town so he reluctantly decided to go to Walmart, even though he had personally protested the building of the very Walmart to which he was headed.

"There's nothing else I can do," he rationalized as he walked through the entrance of the store he hated.

He purchased several large storage bins, a year's supply of non-perishable food, camping and hiking equipment, tools, seeds, clothes, rope, and other items. Andrew was amazed at how clearly he was thinking and how easy it was for him to just cut himself off from the usual "necessities" and focus on what he would actually need in the wilderness.

Andrew had to put the back row of seats down to fit all the supplies in his car. The back seat of his car was usually filled with political paraphernalia but he knew he wouldn't need to save space for that anymore. As he drove away he felt gratitude and relief the trip had saved him time and money.

"I hope I never have the necessity of patronizing such an evil corporation again."

Andrew's thoughts turned to his expedition. He was feeling as energized as he did earlier that morning. He felt like this expedition held all the answers for him. He knew there was something out there for him – something that would change his life forever. Even so, anxious questions did keep creeping into his thoughts.

"How does one just put his life on pause?" he thought. "Will I ever come back? Will I need any of my stuff if I do come back?"

These thoughts and questions filled his mind as he went about his preparation. He drove to several other stores, including the gun shop, picking up items on his list. As he drove he kept the picture of the valley in his mind. Every time he thought of it he had a feeling of peace and calm knowing he was making the right decision. His excitement grew as he came to the end of his list.

When all of the loose ends were tied up, Andrew sat in his car and pondered. He felt like he was missing something important. He poured over his list again attempting to think of something he'd overlooked. He felt that he had enough food to last him until he could figure out how to obtain his own food in the wilderness, he had a tent, warm clothes, two sleeping bags, flashlights with extra batteries, fishing equipment, a rifle with extra ammunition, stove, water purifiers and more.

With his affairs in order, Andrew had left everything he couldn't bring with him to a storage unit, including his Expedition. He spent the evening packing up storage bins and tying up other loose ends. By the end of the night, he had the supplies sorted into 5 large storage bins and two large coolers. At about 9:00 he taped up the last bin and lay down on the floor with a pillow and blanket. He was exhausted. He hadn't rested all day and he had hardly eaten a thing. As he fell asleep on the empty floor of his apartment, he could hardly believe that the next morning he would leave it all behind.

Now, only thirty-six hours later, Andrew *had* left it all behind. Having survived a day of solitude in the wilderness, he lay in his sleeping bag listening to the morning rain hit the tent. He was proud of the accomplishment, but he was mostly proud of his courage in making the decision to leave society and live off the land for a time.

The rain let up, allowing Andrew to arrange the rest of the camp. Once settled, he set out to explore the valley. Andrew had unpacked his thermometer and a few other instruments for recording temperatures, the time of sunrise and sunset, the amount of precipitation each day and any other measurable event or occurrence. He had always wanted to be a scientist so he brought instruments to help him become one.

His camp was located in the Northeastern part of the valley, which he estimated to be about a mile wide and two miles long. Mountains surrounded it except for a break to the southeast where the river flowed. The ascending peaks were tall and some parts were extremely steep. The river ran through the heart of the valley and flowed from a lake to the north of camp, which was about the size of two football fields and not more than fifteen feet in depth.

Andrew hadn't seen many animals since he arrived but as he explored he found tracks and scat. Most of the tracks belonged to deer but there were also some smaller tracks belonging to squirrels, raccoons and other animals.

Exploring, Andrew believed, should always be done in a systematic manner. He divided the valley into eight sections so each day he could explore a section and document his findings. He would start by blazing trails for easy access to each section and then would mark the boundaries.

Food was Andrew's biggest concern. He had plenty of food storage, but he thought he might have to do something else to ensure a good store. He was an excellent fisherman so most of his protein would come from catching trout. Though he despised hunters and hunting, he thought he might have to do a bit of it.

Andrew still worried about something. He left his life in such a hurry he was afraid he had forgotten to bring something or perhaps tie up some loose ends back home. This fear kept nagging at him, but he just assumed it was the same fear everyone had when they left on a road trip, whether it was justified or not.

He went through several survival scenarios to

make sure he had what he would need. The words of his father came ringing into his mind, "you have to prepare to survive. You don't survive by accident."

He froze. His father's words reminded him of the loose end he hadn't tied up - his family. In his rush to get to his destination and make all necessary preparations, he had neglected to call his family members to tell them where he was going and how long he would be there. He had told a few friends, but he wasn't sure his family would be able to get a hold of them to know what had happened.

A wide range of emotions swept over him. He loved his family and wanted to let them know his plans so they wouldn't worry. At the same time, he didn't want to address the defeat. He didn't want their pity or reassurance that everything would be all right. He just wanted to sneak away without dealing with any complications. After all, throughout his adult life dealing with his family had been nothing but complicated.

Although he felt a bit sorry that he didn't tell his family where he was going, he figured they would get the word eventually, whether through his friends or someone else. What really drove him crazy, though, was he knew they would be praying for him every day. He wished they would accept that prayers were worthless and put their trust in things that actually existed.

Andrew refocused himself on the tasks at hand and buried the thoughts of his family.

# Chapter 5: The Struggle

After weeks of recording data and exploring the valley, Andrew wondered if he had made a mistake by coming. He enjoyed the beautiful surroundings and liked feeling as if he was an important part of the environment there, but he was discouraged that he hadn't done anything significant. He hadn't found his place yet.

One cold, cloudy morning, Andrew arose and embarked on one of his usual morning walks. He chose to hike his favorite mountain. Halfway up was an open area where he liked to sit and look out over the valley while eating a simple breakfast. It was a perfect place for meditation and he needed some time to think and ponder. He sat down and looked over the valley. The morning fog hadn't yet lifted, obscuring the tops of the mountains, but he could see the whole valley below.

Having spent three weeks in the wilderness, he was pleased with his ability to obtain food. He had a nice camp with plenty of shelter from the elements. He'd seen a lot of wildlife and established trails where he could hike, make observations and meditate. It was an adjustment going from the frantic pace of the campaign in the city to a quiet and slow wilderness valley. He missed the feeling that there was always something to do in the city. He missed the conversations he had with his friends as they succinctly and clearly laid out the principles that would perfect the world.

They could talk for hours about the personal lives of certain conservative leaders – the stupid things they said, the way they looked, the choices they made, etc. They had a few conservative principles they liked to pick on as well but avoided discussing these by simply concluding that there was no such thing as a substantive conservative idea. These discussions played an important role in reinforcing their ideas and validating their thoughts, particularly because everyone was typically in agreement. None of them could understand how conservative politicians or talk radio personalities even had jobs. They saw their views as representing mainstream America.

They would usually transition to discussing principles and policies that would have particularly significant impacts on the world. Typical discussions included the evils of capitalism and the injustices of the gap between the rich and poor. They discussed ways to even things out and spread the wealth, knowing with a shared inner confidence that the world would be a better place when they succeeded. Global warming and how corporations and the super rich were destroying the planet had been frequent topics in recent months and years. They also shared a mutual disgust for plastic bags, SUVs, two-ply toilet paper, deforestation, guns, Walmart, and everything else to which conservatives thoughtlessly clung.

Back in society Andrew knew his place. He had a purpose – to help others and to make the world a better place. In the wilderness, his only real purpose was to survive and while this was quite important it didn't necessarily keep him busy all day. He needed something else to justify his existence.

Though he had learned much during his time in the wilderness he wondered if he had made a mistake. He was weighed down by the feeling that he was useless.

"Did I act too impulsively? Why am I here? Back home I was important. I solved problems by giving people something they couldn't give themselves. Those people need me more than this valley needs me."

The wilderness seemed to be a complete reversal; in fact, it seemed to function just fine without any help from him. The big bang had put things in motion and everything seemed to be working out naturally. He hadn't studied or observed the animals very closely but they all seemed to do fine on their own. They actually provided food for him and he couldn't survive for long without them. He did not like feeling unneeded or unwanted and he especially deplored the idea of being dependent on something.

Andrew began entertaining the idea that he could just endure the next four years and find a way to push forward the principles in which he believed. He thought that maybe there was still a way to change the world. After all, it really wasn't four years, because the last two years would be spent campaigning. The year leading up to campaigning would be spent planning and searching for the right job so that would take his mind off of the terrible path the country was going down. Besides, the year before that he could collect unemployment and travel and spend time with his friends on the beach somewhere. It wouldn't be too difficult and it sounded a lot better than spending all day alone in the wilderness.

It all made perfect sense. The reason he had his dream was to put things into perspective and help him to see that he did belong in society. He had to spend time in the wilderness to appreciate how valuable he was. He knew people needed his help. He thought back to all the people that had benefited from his efforts over the years. Andrew recalled when he was a young legislative assistant for a congressman in Washington DC and how he helped raspberry farmers in his state obtain a grant. He thought about the unions, the environmental groups, Planned Parenthood, the ACLU and all the other groups he had helped over the years. He didn't remember any particular names or faces of specific people but he knew that his efforts had helped people everywhere. He wanted that feeling of usefulness once again.

Andrew thought it was time to go back home and help more people. He finished his breakfast and started climbing down the mountain and back to his camp. He felt more at peace now that he had made this decision. He already felt useful again. By the simple act of thinking about helping people he was useful. The people he would help did not know it yet but they had just secured a victory. He was officially in their corner again.

There was the concern about what people would say when they realized he was back. He didn't want them to think he was a failure or that he couldn't survive in the wilderness, which would be somewhat embarrassing. However, once they heard of his experience he felt confident they would quickly reach a similar conclusion; that he was too valuable to be secluded in the wilderness.

Andrew decided in the morning he would pack up some of his items and hike out of the mountains and into civilization. It would take about four days to get back and then Arlen could fly back and get the rest of his stuff. He did not like the idea of having to tell Arlen that he couldn't even last a month, but he was a crazy conservative so it didn't really matter what he thought anyway.

Andrew spent the rest of the day gathering items for his departure and preparing for what he might tell people. When he went to bed, he felt like he had made a great decision and that, even though he didn't stay in the wilderness as long as he expected, he still learned from the experience what the universe expected of him.

Wind beat against his tent as Andrew awoke. He was filled with an excitement he hadn't felt since he first arrived in the valley. Emerging from his sleeping bag, he noticed it was quite a bit colder than most mornings.

"Perfect timing. I will get out of here before winter sets in," he thought.

He made some last-minute preparations, ate a quick breakfast and grabbed his backpack. When he unzipped his tent he was hit with a blast of snow. Turning away to cover his face, he managed to zip up the door. Everything outside the tent was white.

"This isn't good," he said to himself. He brushed off the snow and walked to the mesh window in the kitchen. He unzipped the covering to see the entire valley shrouded in snow and the wind swirling everywhere. It was a complete whiteout.

"What now?"

# Chapter 6: The Doe

Emerging from his tent, Andrew gazed upon the reborn valley surrounding him. The daunting mounds of snow had finally melted with the warming weather. Everything looked drastically different than it had when he first arrived. A feeling of new beginnings filled the air.

Though he could feel excitement in the valley, Andrew had already made up his mind to leave. His resolve had been strengthened during the four months he spent cooped up in his tent. With snow up to his waist and no choice but to hunker down and get through the winter it turned out he had just enough food and patience to get through it.

To preserve his sanity, he had forced himself to leave the tent every day, even just for a few minutes. Never wandering far, he managed to do some ice fishing, record the temperature each day and explore a bit, though he spent most of the time in his tent reading and waiting.

The plan was to wait out the winter and then stay in the valley for a few weeks of spring hoping Arlen would stop by with his helicopter. Since the snow was gone, he thought he might as well resume exploring and conducting scientific studies while he waited.

The first spring project was to collect softball-sized rocks and spell "PICK ME UP!" in the dirt just outside his tent. With that in place, he felt could wander away from camp without missing a visit from Arlen.

After a few days of exploring, he returned to the meditation spot on his favorite mountain. The flowers were budding, birds were singing and animals scampered all over the mountain. Andrew enjoyed the ambiance but was not deterred from his plan to leave. He waited an hour, hoping to see Arlen's old helicopter struggling over the mountaintops. An ironic smile crept across his face as he thought about Arlen and his off-white helicopter.

"I never thought I'd be so excited to see that old kook."

With no signs of Arlen, Andrew made his way to the bottom of the mountain and walked on a trail by the river. As he got into the brush something startled him. He heard a sound that he couldn't immediately identify. It did not sound threatening but it seemed out of place.

"Arlen!" Andrew exclaimed out loud. "He's coming to get me. I knew he'd come."

Andrew looked to the sky hoping to see the beat-up helicopter defying gravity and common sense but he didn't see anything. The sound was gone.

"I know I heard something."

Just as he began to wonder if it was gone, he heard the sound again. He still couldn't distinguish it but it seemed to be coming from the river, not the sky. He walked slowly toward the water. As he drew closer he stopped and listened. Amongst the trickle and steady flow of the river he thought he heard splashing.

The sound grew louder and then stopped. Andrew pushed aside some brush and inched closer to the bank. He was anxious about the sound but curiosity had overtaken him. Parting the brush in front of him, he crept forward quietly.

Once in clear view, he was surprised to see a deer thrashing furiously in the middle of the river. Deer were normally graceful and smooth, but this deer was neither. She was a doe of medium size with light brown fur, large ears and black eyes full of terror.

"What on earth?" he whispered.

The river was fairly shallow where she stood and the water moved slowly. Other deer had bounded through this river in roughly the same spot many times over the past weeks with no trouble.

Andrew watched the doe closely. She was struggling with her upper body as she lifted her front legs into the air and then splashed them down into the water. She would stand still for a minute or so and then thrash again. Andrew wondered if she might be playing a game but her violent movements and erratic behavior suggested she was in trouble.

He inched forward to get a better look. As the deer started lurching again, he could see that at least one of her hind legs was stuck.

"She's caught on something, but what is it?"

Without hesitating he stepped off the bank and into the river. The glacial water stung his legs and feet and almost instantly made them feel like ice blocks. He had taken a few steps when the doe spotted him. Panic flashed in her eyes and she fought more fervently. Andrew put up both hands and tried to calm her.

"Don't worry. I'm not going to hurt you. I'm here to help! I want to help you! Calm down; it's okay."

The doe arched violently to get away from Andrew and whatever imprisoned her leg. She struggled to the point of exhaustion until she could splash no more. She panted heavily. Taking advantage of her weakened state, Andrew moved closer. She waited until he was within five feet and tried to thrash some more, but it was no use; her strength was gone. Once it was clear she had accepted defeat, he moved toward her again.

A look of complete helplessness was in the doe's large black eyes as if she had already consigned herself to death. Andrew slowly reached out with his palms to comfort her. He touched the top of her hind leg and patted her fur. Having no strength left, her only response was a slight tremor. She was at Andrew's mercy.

Cautiously stepping closer, Andrew battled to keep his footing in the icy current. Though his feet were nearly numb, he felt something touch the top of his right foot. Sliding forward, he realized there was a log on the bed of the river. With another step forward, he discovered another log running parallel with the first. Reaching into the water, he felt small gaps between the logs. The deer's back left leg was stuck between the two logs.

He thrust both hands into the water to feel where the deer was stuck. Inching his hands along the logs, he reached her leg. He was nearly out of breath but was determined to see how much space there was between the leg and the logs. At that moment the deer began moving her leg furiously to try to break free. Andrew's finger got pinched between the deer's leg and the log. Feeling his touch, the doe raised her free leg and kicked Andrew squarely in the shoulder.

Cursing and writhing he jerked out of the water. The pain was excruciating!

"What's wrong with you?" He screamed while holding his shoulder. "I'm trying to save you and you kick me! What kind of stupid animal -"

Andrew's shoulder was throbbing and he was shivering from the glacial water that now soaked his entire body.

"I've got to get out of here," he thought. "The sooner I can get back to my life the better. These animals have no idea what's good for them. I've had it."

Andrew was more ready than ever to get home. The animals didn't respect or care about him. He was ready to give up when the deer thrashed again, evidently still concerned that Andrew was going to harm her.

"I'm not going to hurt you!" he yelled. "How stupid are you? If I were going to hurt you I would have done it already. You're not worth saving."

He turned his back to the doe, took a step toward his camp and then paused. Andrew had lost interest in helping but now wanted her to see how stupid she was for fearing him. He had to let her know he was trying to save her; not harm her. Lunging into the river again, he quickly found the logs again. About as thick as a telephone pole; they were slippery and heavy, making them nearly impossible to move.

Despite his best efforts he couldn't separate them.

"There must be a spot where the gap is wider."

Andrew followed the narrow gap from the deer's leg to the left and found a widening in the gap where her leg could fit. He grabbed her leg firmly, inched it toward the wider gap and managed to pull it through the gap. Feeling freedom in her leg again she burst out of the water. As she sprang away she kicked Andrew in the chin. He winced and grabbed his chin with his hands.

Turning to curse again, he was struck by what he saw. She was frantically, but now smoothly, hopping through the river. His pain seemed to subside as he watched the beautiful creature effortlessly bounce to the shore. He couldn't believe this was the same deer that had looked so frightened and so defeated only moments before. She had a noticeable limp in her step, but she still moved with mesmerizing grace.

The doe worked her way to the opposite bank, stepped out of the water and paused. Her leg was covered in blood. She looked back at Andrew for an extended moment, and then bounded toward a ridge on the far side of the river. Though clearly fatigued from the ordeal, she managed to jump over bushes and rocks as she fled.

Just as she was about to disappear over the ridge she stopped. Andrew watched intently and his heart seemed to pause as he waited to see what she would do.

The doe stood motionless for a second, looking at the surroundings on the other side of the ridge. Having scanned the area she seemed convinced that no danger existed and looked as if she would proceed down the jagged rocks into the cover of trees. Before disappearing, she glanced back at Andrew. Then, dipping her head toward the ground and up toward the sky, she stared at him for long moment, then turned and regally faded into the brush.

Andrew shivered in silence. His body was drenched in freezing cold water but he couldn't take his eyes off of the spot from which she disappeared.

"I can't believe it!" he thought to himself. "I just saved a deer. She would have died without me. She had no chance."

He didn't know what to make of what he'd done. It seemed like it lasted a few hours, but only took a few adrenaline-filled minutes. He had experienced such an intense thrill as he helped the struggling deer get untangled. With delight and pain he had felt transcendent as the freed deer trampled him and bounded away.

The entire episode produced a rush of adrenalin and such a high that he felt like he was soaring in the clouds. Thoughts and emotions swirled around him as he stared back at where the doe had disappeared.

"You're welcome!" He yelled as loud as he could.

He could no longer see the doe, but he felt like she could hear him.

"Maybe I am needed here," he thought. "She would have died without me. Maybe this is my true calling. I'm not here just to study temperatures and partake of the beauty; I am here to give. I'm here to help. My job is one of service and sacrifice for the benefit of animals, plants and all living things within this valley. Science sent me here to not only study and react to the forces, but to interact with the forces. I am an ambassador to nature."

The skills and talents he gained in his political career were perfectly suited to such an endeavor. His career was all about serving and helping those who couldn't help themselves. His whole satisfaction in life came from being an ambassador to the poor, the oppressed and the afflicted. Ever since his initial attempt to help the beavers, he had convinced himself there was no such need for his skills in the wilderness, but now he realized he had been wrong. He had probably just overlooked opportunities in nature because he just assumed everything was all right.

The doe's struggle was a sign from nature that it needed him to help with the animals.

"What about the people back in society who need my help?" he wondered. "Who will help them and stand up for them? They need me too."

## LIBERAL IN NATURE

He pondered as he retraced his steps to the edge of the river. Gazing back at the spot where the doe had been stuck, he reflected on his time in the valley, wondering if this new path held his ultimate destiny in the valley. Suddenly, his shivering body felt a jolt of warmth from inside. His body tingled and the hair on his neck stood up. He felt love and warmth and he knew the answer.

"Thank you, Big Bang," he said, looking up into the sky. "You have never led me astray."

Feeling was starting come back to his feet as he walked along the trail back to camp. Though he knew what he was to do, his mind was still conflicted.

"The people back in society need me, but there are other enlightened individuals who can do the job. They can keep an eye on things while I am gone. But if I leave the valley, no one will be here when a deer gets stuck in the river or when some animal gets into trouble."

Walking back to his camp briskly, he made up his mind. Though his body was shivering and the pain was setting in more with each minute, he felt euphoric.

"I have been fixing society for so long; it is now time to fix nature. I have to stay! It would be selfish not to."

# Chapter 7: The Robin

*At sunrise on a clear blue day, a mother robin returns to her nest where five hungry chicks await. She has spent the early morning hours searching for food for her babies. She, though hungry herself, saved the first fruits of her labors for her little ones. As she flies back to the nest to greet and feed her precious offspring, she is troubled. A fear that has been growing inside her heart for many days is about to be realized. She doesn't know why, but she knows the time is right.*

*She finds her nest effortlessly and lands amongst her chirping young. They eagerly call for breakfast not knowing what awaits them in only a few minutes. The caring mother regurgitates the worms she found and places the nutritious meal into the mouths of her young. When she is finished feeding her baby chicks, she nudges them to the edge of the nest. It's time to learn to fly.*

Since Andrew didn't find any other immediate crises that needed attending to, he decided the best way to help the animals was to know their needs inside and out. He spent the next few weeks researching and gathering data about the animals; their food sources, habits and patterns. He noticed that some squirrels were fatter than others and decided to investigate. Some animals lived closer to the river than others forcing many to travel farther to get water. He also observed that some trees grew taller than others and had more opportunities to thrive and grow. His keen sense of justice was incensed.

Nature was a harsh and unforgiving place so Andrew decided to make it more fair and balanced. There wasn't anyone to help the weak animals. Everything was left to chance and pedigree. If an animal was born with a weakness, there wasn't anyone to level the playing field. He was determined to change that by bringing more hope to the valley.

Andrew threw himself into his new observations immediately. Keeping a journal of all his findings, he came up with several ideas of how to best serve the valley. All of his new ideas filled him with purpose and hope. He was amazed at how he had overlooked so many inequalities. He had allowed himself to be overly impressed by the way nature worked, blinding him to the necessary improvement. Where once he saw beauty and harmony he now saw unfairness and imperfection. He saw opportunities to serve and right the wrongs imposed by nature.

"If God is real, loving and perfect he would not allow such things to happen," Andrew thought. "*Science* has created the world and is still perfecting it. That is what evolution is all about. But evolution is a slow solution unless there is some positive force that can help speed it up. I am that force. I can't let nature down; I will right wrongs, heal wounds, fight unfairness and bring equality. I can make sure all animals get equal amounts of food and water and provide all the trees an even amount of sunlight."

Andrew knew it was an enormous challenge but he loved the valley and would do everything he could to make it better; using the same tactics he'd used in politics and striving to get the same results. For the first time since his arrival, he was truly proud of the valley.

Thinking back to the dream that had sent him there, Andrew realized that the perfection and beauty he saw was not reality but what could become so with his help. It was a vision – a glimpse – of what science beckoned him to do. It was his destiny to turn this valley into the place he saw in his dream. This would become a utopia.

Andrew woke up every morning at sunrise and

found a quiet place on a hill overlooking the river and lake to observe the animals' behavior. He knew it would take time to learn their habits and gain their trust, but was confident he would succeed as he started fundamentally transforming the valley into an idyllic model of perfect harmony.

After the morning feeding he would watch the animals retreat to their homes and then go over his morning observations to look for patterns. In the afternoon he hiked around the valley taking additional notes and making observations. After resting and eating, he would head out just before dusk to watch the animals come back for water. When darkness came he would retreat to his tent and record his final conclusions of the day.

This pattern continued for many weeks as brilliant insights enlightened his mind about all the recurring problems in the valley. He was careful not to overstep his bounds with the animals but knew in the near future it was necessary to take a more active role in the valley's patterns. For fairness to be achieved, someone had to step into that role and make it happen. Deep in his heart, he felt certain he was the right person for the job.

Andrew was making his usual rounds one morning when he found a baby robin struggling on the ground below a tree a few hundred yards from camp. The robin was hopping around on the ground.

Andrew watched it struggle for a few minutes and was immediately taken in by its fluffy feathers and petite size. The robin was trying to flap its wings but couldn't lift itself off the ground. With every jump and flap of wings it would return softly back to earth.

"It must have accidently fallen out of the nest."

Looking up, Andrew noticed a nest in a tree about ten feet above him. He listened for chirping but heard none. Andrew felt it needed to be returned to the nest so it could gain strength and learn to fly.

Taking off his shirt, Andrew was careful not to directly touch the robin. The mother might reject it if it had his scent. He put his hands inside his shirt and approached the robin slowly and quietly. The robin was still jumping frantically trying to get off the ground. As Andrew got closer the robin stopped hopping and looked at Andrew suspiciously. Andrew inched closer with his hands outstretched inside his shirt. The Robin hopped away.

When the robin calmed down, Andrew approached again but it hopped away playfully. This happened a dozen times until the robin appeared so fatigued it could hardly hop. Andrew got closer and closer until he was finally able to pick up the robin with his shirt. He held it gently and looked closely at its face and wings. It had full feathers, tiny little talons and a puny beak. He was amazed at how small it was.

"A little guy like you shouldn't be hopping around the forest. You'll end up as breakfast."

Andrew reconsidered what he should do with the tiny bird. Leaving it to hop around on the ground was not an option.

"What am I going to do with you?" he asked the robin. "Should I take you back to my camp? Should I put you in your nest? Should I toss you in the air to help you learn to fly?"

"If I take you back to camp you might never experience what other birds experience. However, I could protect you from danger and provide food. You wouldn't have to worry about flying around, being the early bird, struggling for food or worrying about predators. I could give you everything you need. You wouldn't even have to learn to fly if you didn't want to. You could run around like a chicken, for all I care. Maybe you were born this way. There is no rule that you have to be a flying bird. You can be whatever kind of bird you want to be. Maybe Mother Nature made you to not fly. Penguins don't fly and they do just fine."

"If I put you in your nest you might have a chance to get stronger and fly. Of course, then you will have a life of struggle and toil. Who will provide for you then? If you fly off, I won't be able to help you and no one else will. You will face predators and starvation. Your life will constantly be in danger. And what if I return you and your mother won't take you back into the nest? I don't want you to face that kind of rejection."

"If I throw you in the air, you may be able to figure out how to fly, but you will land hard on the ground many times. I couldn't bear to watch you crash to the earth and get injured, even if it means you might learn to fly by doing it. And then, if you did learn to fly, you would have to deal with all of those other things with no one to protect you."

"Your parents have obviously abandoned you and don't have the compassion to find you or help you. You have been abandoned, but not by me. I will take you to my camp and raise you there. I will find worms and seeds for you. It will be great and you will be safer there than anywhere else in the wilderness."

Andrew marched back to camp feeling inspired to have saved another helpless animal from the dangers of nature.

"I will call you Rob," Andrew said softly. "Don't worry, I won't abandon you or try to tell you what type of bird you should be. You can be a frog for all I care."

He put Rob in the tent while he gathered twigs and soft grass to make a nest. Returning, he noticed that Rob had pooped in his tent so he emptied a bin and put him inside as a temporary shelter. He didn't have enough sticks and grass to completely cover the bottom of the bin so he padded one side.

Andrew was deeply pleased he had saved Rob from predators and from the harsh world. He looked forward to having a little companion.

# Chapter 8: The Trees

*The forest is a world of compromise and balance. The trees reach for sunlight, but they know their limits. Some trees grow tall and some stay short – all part of nature's plan. Not all trees are meant for the canopies and some aren't ready for the direct rays of sunshine. Others are meant to grow tall with balanced branches stretching out in all directions.*

*There is only so much sunlight. There is a limited amount of water. The soil can only provide for a certain number of roots. The trees know their roles and they fill the measure of their creation.*

Early summer painted the valley with fully formed leaves and grasses. Andrew loved the warmth and beauty of summer. There was a carefree feeling in the valley and Andrew soaked it in as much as he could, even relaxing his daily routine a bit.

# LIBERAL IN NATURE

In the early morning he would dig up some worms for Rob, record the temperature and eat some breakfast. In the afternoon he would sometimes take a short walk but occasionally would just hang around his camp. He didn't go on many challenging hikes because he needed to stay close to Rob. He loved just being around his camp where he could take naps, play with Rob and watch the other animals.

Camp was perfectly situated for Andrew's purposes. The trees above his tent provided excellent shade, allowing him to lounge in his camping chairs without dealing with the direct sunlight.

One day while admiring the trees Andrew noticed that three shorter trees above his tent were shaded by one large tree. He had always loved the trees near his camp but never really studied their circumstance.

The largest tree stood about a hundred feet tall with long branches stretching in all directions. The branches had leaves that contributed to most of the shade Andrew enjoyed. However, there were three smaller trees that grew in the shadow of the large tree. These trees were about half the size of the large tree. Andrew didn't know what types of trees they were, but he felt bad for them.

"Why should they have to grow in another tree's shadow? They don't have an opportunity to become all they can be."

While admiring the tall tree, he wondered if

perhaps it had grown a bit *too* tall. After all, it was taking up all the sunlight and not leaving any for the other trees. The other trees looked like they wanted to grow bigger but couldn't because the large tree was depriving them of their chances to grow.

"I guess I better do something," Andrew said, sensing another call from nature.

He didn't want to cut down the tall tree entirely, but felt he needed to regulate it enough to allow the others to thrive also. He wanted the smaller trees to get some direct sunlight so they could photosynthesize on equal terms with the large tree.

Andrew had purchased a saw from Walmart but hadn't used it. This was the right opportunity. He threw a rope over the lowest branch of the large tree and pulled himself up. He then climbed up the tree a bit and identified a few of the biggest branches that were responsible for blocking sunlight from the smaller trees.

Andrew went to work cutting off the oppressive sun-blocking branches. It took a few minutes to get through each one. Once he cut through, it would fall to the ground taking out other branches below it.

Andrew cut off five large branches and a few others were incidentally knocked down in the process. He felt sorry for the large tree. He didn't want to drastically change it, but he knew it was better for all the trees if he helped it adjust to an immediate and more important need. He knew if one tree got too big, it had to sacrifice to help the other trees. It was a duty each tree owed to the other trees.

"The forest is more important than a single tree," he said to reassure the tall tree. "Wear it like a badge of honor."

When Andrew completed his work, he climbed down the side that still had branches and looked up to survey his work. Andrew still had perfect shade, but now the smaller trees accounted for a larger portion of it. The smaller trees were now receiving direct sunlight too, which made Andrew excited for them.

"Now you can thrive!" he exclaimed.

The tall tree was still mighty; it now had a large space with no branches in the middle. It was still beautiful and still towered over the other trees. Andrew knew that, given greater opportunities, the smaller trees would probably outgrow the tall tree and push it aside.

"That's how nature works," Andrew said apologetically to the tall tree. "We all have to step aside at some point to let others have opportunities. It's the natural cycle. I don't want to interfere with that."

Andrew spent the afternoon basking in the shade of *all* the trees as a personal reward. As the sun shifted positions in the afternoon, he noticed that the smaller trees were no longer getting direct sunlight.

He made a few more trips up the large tree to trim and eventually the small trees had direct sunlight throughout most of the day.

Andrew brought Rob outside to see what he had done. Rob bounced around happily in the shade. Andrew gave him a worm and put him back in his bin inside the tent.

# Chapter 9: The Apples

*Struggling for food is a way of life for the animals. They must find whatever they can in order to survive. If they don't find enough nourishment, they risk becoming weak and dying of starvation or becoming prey. The struggle keeps them moving and searching. The struggle is what keeps them strong.*

As the summer progressed, Andrew started wandering away from his camp more and more. Rob was growing bigger and Andrew felt like he could handle himself in his bin for longer periods of time.

One afternoon as Andrew was exploring the valley he came across a small apple orchard. He thought it was strange that apples would be growing in the wilderness and that there would be multiple trees in such a small area, as if they had been planted there.

He walked over to the orchard and noticed that apples were already growing on the branches. He took one and tasted it. It tasted a bit sour and he determined that it was probably not ripe yet. He noticed deer tracks covering the ground below the trees.

"They must enjoy the apples," he thought. "But how do they reach the high branches?"

Andrew returned to the apple orchard that evening to see if the deer would eat the apples. He found a spot about fifty yards away so he could watch them without interfering.

About an hour before dusk he noticed that some deer were wandering toward the orchard. There were six does and two fawns. He watched as they approached the trees and began searching for apples. Most of the apples on the low-hanging branches were gone so they had to stretch their necks to reach the higher ones. The deer struggled to reach the apples and only a few of the taller ones were able to reach. The fawns just bounced around since they couldn't reach any apples.

Andrew remembered when he was in elementary school and how he wanted to be a basketball player. He wasn't as tall as the other kids and he had trouble getting the ball to the basket, while most of the other kids had no trouble shooting layups.

He didn't think it was fair that he was shorter than

# LIBERAL IN NATURE

the others; after all, he wanted to make baskets just as much as them – if not more. He would complain to his mom and she would tell him, "God made you your size for a reason. There is always a reason."

"What a crock!" Andrew said to himself, as the childhood memory flashed before him. "God never did anything to help me, just like He is not helping these deer. But *I* will help them!"

The next day Andrew returned just before dusk. The deer hadn't arrived yet so he hurried to the orchard. He started jumping up and down knocking apples to the ground. When there were about twenty apples on the ground he ran off to his observation spot to see what the deer would do.

The deer returned to the trees about the same time as the previous day. Upon discovering the apples on the ground, they immediately started feasting. Andrew swelled with pride as he watched the two fawns chomping away at the apples. He felt privileged that he had provided nourishment for them. He hoped they appreciated it.

"But they have no idea that I did this for them. For all they know, these apples just fell because it was windy." He thought to himself. "How do I let them know that *I* helped them? I want them to know the source of their dinner so they will trust me."

The next afternoon Andrew returned to the orchard with his backpack. He shook the bases of several trees to get apples to fall; then he picked up the apples that would fit in his backpack and carried it back to his camp.

When he got to his camp Andrew made several piles of apples about thirty yards from his tent. When evening came Andrew sat in one of his camp chairs to see if any deer would feast on his apples. He waited until dark and didn't see any deer.

The next morning when he awoke, Andrew noticed that the apple piles were gone. He was glad some deer had found them, but he wanted to be there when they did. He got more apples and made similar piles.

Again, he waited for deer to come that evening and none came. He was disappointed so he walked to the orchard and discovered that the deer were there, eating apples off the ground. This made Andrew upset. He had gone to so much trouble to gather the apples and put them in piles and the deer were still coming to the orchard. He noticed that there were no more apples on branches low enough for the deer, so they were relying solely on the apples that had fallen.

The next morning, Andrew woke up at dawn to see if the deer would eat his apples. As light hit the valley, he saw the same group of deer from the orchard making their way to his piles. They found his apples and ate until they were gone. Andrew tried to make some noise every few minutes so they would see him and connect the dots between him and the apples. He couldn't tell if it was effective, but he was glad they enjoyed the meal.

That afternoon Andrew made several trips to the orchard with his backpacks. He didn't want any apples to fall randomly anymore so he picked every apple from the trees and carried them back to his camp. He put most of them in his tent and the rest he made into piles for the deer. Because it was impossible to predict when and how many apples would fall from a tree, he decided to make a system that would be more certain for the deer. He didn't want the deer to count on finding apples on the ground only to find there weren't any. He felt that if he controlled the system, the deer would be better off.

That evening the deer didn't come to his camp. Andrew found them at the orchard, but with no apples to eat, they seemed confused and disappointed. This gave Andrew hope. He knew they must be hungry for apples and he was the only one with the apples so they would eventually have to rely on him. He knew that if he could get them to be hungry, he could earn their trust.

The next morning the deer came to his camp and ate his apples. That night they returned again to eat the apples. Andrew knew he had won their loyalty. He continued doing this morning and night and the deer kept returning. Every time Andrew formed the piles, he moved them a few yards closer to his camp.

This continued for a few weeks. Eventually the piles were only about fifteen feet from his camp. The deer – though cautious – didn't seem to mind where the piles were as long as there was food. They would approach carefully but still came to eat the apple piles each day.

After two weeks of making the apple piles, Andrew realized the apples in his tent were starting to rot. He had picked all the apples but he wasn't able to give them away fast enough. That evening, Andrew decided to take all the remaining apples and pile them for the deer. They came and ate them all.

The next morning, Andrew awoke at dawn to see if the deer had returned. He unzipped his tent window and saw them all standing where the piles usually were. They looked around and sniffed the ground, as if waiting for something. Andrew zipped up the window and went back to bed.

When he awoke the second time, Andrew unzipped the window to see that the deer were still waiting. Annoyance set in.

"I have fed you for two weeks straight," he thought. "Isn't that good enough for you?"

Andrew stayed in his tent until all the deer went away. He hadn't thought about what he would do when there were no apples left. Things were fine when there were apples to go around, but now they were gone and he didn't know what to do. All he had wanted to do was gain their trust.

"Now that I've got their trust, I have to keep it," he realized.

He set out with his backpacks to gather other food for the deer. He had seen them feeding on green leaves and clovers so he picked as much as he could and stored the harvest in his tent. He thought he had enough to last a week or so.

Andrew focused on picking food in the areas where the deer usually fed. He knew if he could limit the food they could get on their own, they would have to come to him for more.

Each morning and night he set out piles of whatever he had picked. The deer returned several times a day to eat the piles. Eventually, they started bedding down closer to Andrew's tent.

Upon laying out a pile, Andrew would whistle and the deer would emerge from their beds to feast. Andrew felt his plan was working. The deer were increasingly friendly to him. At times, they would even follow him on his hikes, hoping to get some food from him. Usually, however, they just bedded down near his tent and came out to get food.

The deer still had to go to the river or lake to get water so Andrew set up some water pots near the food piles. Each day he would carry the pots to the river to get fresh water. The deer then had everything they needed right by his tent.

This continued throughout the summer. Between the deer and Rob, Andrew was extremely busy gathering food and water.

Rob's appetite was growing and Andrew spent a significant amount of time looking for worms. He dug for them on the banks of the river and near the lake. Rob was becoming quite a hopper, which made Andrew proud of him.

Andrew was also proud of his work with the trees in his camp. He did notice, however, that the smaller trees' leaves were extremely dry. He worried they were not getting enough water so he started carrying bucket loads of water from the river and dumping them at the base of the smaller trees. He didn't think the tall tree needed any water.

## Chapter 10: The Bear

*It is the regulator of the forest. It is a predator to some and a protector to others. It is both carnivore and omnivore; playful and dangerous; curious and ruthless; cunning and simple. The bear does what it wants and what the bear wants is good for the valley.*

*As long as the bear inhabits the valley, other predators keep their distance. The bear gives back nutrients – salmon, honey, berries – to the forest, which seeps into the soil and streams. It is essential to the well being of the valley and its inhabitants.*

The weather improved more and more during the summer. The high temperature was usually in the upper seventies and it felt perfect to Andrew. Spring had been nice, but had still been a bit cool with rain nearly every day. Summer was proving to be just the right temperature with plenty of sunshine. The valley looked beautiful and the animals seemed happy.

Andrew looked forward to swimming everyday in the river or lake. He forgot to pack a swimsuit, so he usually just went in the nude. The water was always cold, but after a few minutes he would get used to it. He loved the feeling of freedom as he swam through the water. It felt so natural.

The feeling of unencumbered freedom prompted Andrew to become a nudist. Being natural seemed only right since he was trying to become one with the natural living organisms. It took him a few days to get over his self-consciousness of walking around naked in broad daylight. Andrew wondered what someone might say if they hiked through the valley, but that possibility seemed unlikely, so he became bolder with his nudity.

Andrew was more satisfied than ever with his wilderness adventure. He felt in tune with nature, which made him happy. Helping nature had brought pride and joy that he never imagined it would, which made him want to serve more. He continually looked for more opportunities to help the plants and animals, improving everything around him.

Andrew hoped that walking around barefoot for a few days would toughen the soles of his feet, but found it quite difficult to make his daily rounds without shoes so he allowed himself that comfort – for the valley's sake.

## LIBERAL IN NATURE

After a few days of being a shoe-wearing nudist, he decided it was also very uncomfortable to sit down on his bare butt to make observations. His skin was irritated in several areas and it generally was not enjoyable to navigate the valley without clothes. Since cotton and wool are natural products, he reasoned, he could still be one with nature while wearing clothes made from these products. So, he reduced his nudity to swimming only.

One morning while swimming in the river, Andrew noticed a few deer standing by the shore, watching him eagerly. Andrew remembered he had forgotten to fill up their water pots for the day. He wondered why they didn't just drink from the river in front of them, but nonetheless determined to fill the pots when he was done swimming.

A few minutes into his swim, Andrew heard something rustling in the bushes. He was so used to deer coming and going that he hardly paid any attention to it. He nearly let out a scream when he saw a large brown bear emerging from the bushes and walking toward the water.

The bear approached the river at a steady pace without taking interest in any other animals. It walked toward the deer who nervously backed away as it drew near. The bear walked with its head down, only occasionally looking up to give the animals a harsh look, as if to say "you better get out of my way!" As it neared the edge of the stream, the deer turned and ran.

The bear stepped into the stream boldly and stood for a moment looking up at the fleeing deer. Seemingly not intent on scaring them away, it also didn't go out of its way to make the other animals feel comfortable. With a bellow, it stuck its nose into the water.

This was Andrew's first encounter with a bear since coming to the valley. He had seen several bears while fishing in Alaska, but was usually in a boat when he saw them. Andrew had a mixture of fear and awe for such large, powerful creatures. As he watched the bear loudly gulping the water, however, he became increasingly annoyed.

Watching closely, he slowly swam backward until he reached the opposite shore. Andrew was appalled at the bear's arrogance in approaching the river, scaring the deer and ignoring him.

"Who does he think he is? Why should he be able to dictate what all the other animals do? Just because he's bigger than the rest and has sharp claws and teeth doesn't mean he can boss everyone around. It's not fair. The other animals should be able to drink from that stream whenever they want without having to worry about being bullied. Bullies don't ever think about others; only themselves."

The bear sat down in the water and looked around

as if waiting for something. He patted the water with his paw, dunked his head and then walked around looking in the river as if searching for something. The other animals kept a safe distance and did not return to the water. They watched the bear for a while, then turned and walked away.

This encounter with the bear infuriated Andrew. The blatant arrogance was too much to handle. It wasn't fair that the bear could show up at the river when all the other animals were drinking and enjoying themselves and just force them to leave. He wished the deer would stand up to him and make it clear he can't bully them. The deer didn't defend themselves, so Andrew had to.

He got out of the river and yelled at the bear. It hardly paid any attention to him so he cursed at it and told it to go away. The bear didn't flinch. Andrew was about fifty yards away and, not wanting to get any closer, he decided to throw some rocks at it.

The first few rocks fell well short. He threw a couple more that landed closer but the bear didn't budge. The next rock landed only a few feet away splashing the bear's face with water. The bear suddenly turned its huge head in Andrew's direction and, standing up on hind legs, rose high out of the water. It then hunched back down on all fours and started moving menacingly toward Andrew.

Andrew dropped the rocks and started backing

away slowly. The bear had probably had enough for one day so Andrew chose to give him a break. Besides, he didn't see many other good options. Maybe he'd caught the bear on a bad day and should give him another chance. When it stopped lumbering toward him, he turned around and ran back to camp as fast as he could.

That evening Andrew thought about the bear and kept his eye out just in case it decided to check out his camp. Andrew made sure that he didn't leave any food out in the open and went to bed early, exhausted with the day's excitement.

When Andrew woke up, thoughts of the bear immediately came to mind.

"Even if it was just a bad day, there's no excuse for that kind of arrogance. What a bully!"

Andrew hated bullies. It reminded him of a time in eighth grade when a bully named Evan had terrorized the other kids. He only picked on Andrew a few times but it was enough for Andrew to hate him.

Remembering one instance in gym class made Andrew shudder. All of the boys were showering after gym class when a scrawny little seventh grader reluctantly entered the shower and began washing himself off. Evan somehow made showering with other boys more difficult and traumatic than it already was. Andrew had learned to wait for Evan to be done with his shower before he would take his, even if it meant being late for his next class.

The scrawny seventh grader hadn't learned that lesson and chose a shower a few feet away from Evan. Whistling and cat calling the boy produced nothing, as he turned and ignored the taunts. Evan, clearly annoyed that he wasn't getting a reaction, turned toward the boy and urinated on him. Evan laughed as the boy quickly moved to another shower to clean off. The boy then ran out of the shower and to his locker with tears in his eyes while Evan laughed and whistled. The horrifying memory had been seared into Andrew's mind.

It wasn't that he had inflicted physical harm that bothered Andrew; it was the way he made people *feel* that bothered him. Evan made people feel so helpless and small. Most of all, Evan had prematurely destroyed Andrew's belief that people in the world are innately good. Several years later, this still bothered him as he still tried to reconcile his basic belief in the goodness of people with the behavior of the bully. He hated Evan for even making him think of such things.

Andrew worried the bear's bullying would destroy the confidence of the deer and they wouldn't be the same thereafter. He didn't like anyone to experience that feeling of smallness and helplessness. He determined it was his duty to level the playing field and put the bear in his place. He named the bear

Evan so he would never forget what the bear truly was.

Andrew fretted that Evan might cause problems with other animals or that Rob might wander off and become a victim of the bear's voracious appetite. The bear's constant clawing of trees could damage them or even destroy them. The amount of harm Evan could do was almost limitless.

"He has ruled these parts long enough. It's time other animals had the same opportunities. Someone has the regulate."

While Andrew was worrying about Evan, he noticed Rob suddenly flapping his wings and lifting off the ground. He was airborne for a few seconds before gently falling back to earth. Instantly trying again, he flew for a few seconds more.

Rob seemed ecstatic he was finally able to fly. Andrew, however, worried that he might fly off to his death, especially with Evan lurking out in the wild. He loved Rob and wanted him to stay at his camp so he put Rob back in the tent to keep him safe. Rob started flying around the tent and could stay airborne for several minutes, eventually.

Andrew didn't want to lose his friend so he kept him in the tent until he could get stronger. Andrew knew the dangers that awaited Rob in the outside world, but his helpless friend had no idea what was out there. Andrew knew that Rob depended on him for food and safety and it was in Rob's best interest to stay close to Andrew. He loved him too much to let him go.

# Chapter 11: The Wolf

*The sleek creature crept quietly upon a small herd of deer. Silently he watched as the deer grazed in the meadow. The herd consisted of six does and a buck with no fawns. Knowing he couldn't bring down a buck on his own, he watched carefully for any sign of weakness among the does. Patiently, he waited and watched. He knew the signals – a stumble, a limp, discolored fur, signs of blood. He almost didn't need to look; he could just sense weakness through some ancient gene he possessed.*

*The deer browsed the grass. A few of them paused and looked around nervously every minute or two. He thought they may have sensed his presence but waited patiently. Suddenly, the deer got anxious and huddled closer together. They continued feeding but he was certain they knew danger lurked.*

*One doe, however, did not heed the warnings. She*

*continued feeding in a line away from the herd. The creature zeroed in on her. He knew those animals that were not alert to dangers around them were usually impaired in some way. The doe continued to feed when the creature spotted it; blood on her leg.*

One warm summer morning, Andrew watched six does drink from his water pots. He noticed they all looked fatter than they had a few months prior. He wondered if he was giving them too many calories or if the portions were too large.

"I will have to cut down the portion size. Maybe I should force them to get some exercise. I could run through their bedding area yelling 'get moving!' I don't want them to be scared of me so I'll wait and see what happens the next few months.

Andrew noticed that the does seemed uneasy about something. They normally walked and drank casually, but this morning they seemed twitchy and anxious. He wondered if there was too much dirt or algae in the water he had provided. When they were done, he would get some fresh water from the river. As he made his plan for the afternoon, he noticed something move in a small grove of trees about a hundred yards from the deer. The object looked gray and moved slowly.

Andrew waited eagerly for the creature to appear. He desperately hoped that it was what he thought it was. He had loved wolves since childhood when his uncle had given him a poster of a wolf for one of his birthdays. The poster showed a wolf leaning back on its hind legs with eyes intensely focused straight ahead and fangs protruding from his mouth. Andrew had hung the picture up in his room and studied it often. At first he was afraid of it. The teeth frightened him and the eyes of the creature looked eerie and unpredictable. On dark nights, he couldn't look at the picture. At times he even covered it with a sheet.

Over time, however, he convinced himself that the wolf was not dangerous. The wolf's eyes were not eerie, but merely misunderstood. After all, it wasn't the wolf's fault that he evolved with those eyes. The fangs were not really dangerous, but simply defense mechanisms to defend the wolf from those who would seek to do it unjust harm. He had even imagined positive and constructive ways the wolf could use the fangs; opening soda cans, two-hole punching paper, aerating the lawn and making whiffle balls.

In his dreams, he rode on the wolf's back, as if protected from the cold with his warm coat of fur. Through those years, he developed a bond with the wolf and felt the wolf protected him. He named his childhood friend, "Gray Protector".

It was because of this early bond he had developed with Gray Protector that he fought so hard to get wolves reintroduced into the wild in his state. He encouraged his Congressman to get involved in the issue and he was the legislative assistant who helped draft language to bring the wolves back. He faced opposition from ignorant farmers, bigoted ranchers, and intolerant parents who thought the wolves were dangerous, but the legislation passed.

He debunked reports from farmers that wolves had killed livestock and threatened their businesses. Not only did he fight to get wolves back, but he also successfully included language in the legislation punishing anyone who harmed a wolf. It was a proud moment for him, because for so many years Gray Protector had kept him safe, but now *he* was the protector. He believed that even the simpleton farmers, who were so full of hatred and suspicion, would eventually see how great the wolves were and that they could all peacefully coexist.

In all his work with wolves, Andrew had never seen a real wolf in person and now, as this sleek looking animal emerged from the trees, he finally got his chance. It looked a bit heavier than Gray Protector, but they bore a striking resemblance. An unexpected fear and uneasy premonition flooded Andrew as he watched the wolf edge along the trees, stalking something. He quickly suppressed this fear.

He felt certain there was nothing to fear and even felt ashamed for passing prejudicial judgment on the wolf. It was a creature just like the deer, but nobody feared deer.

"Why do they get such a bad rap?"

Wolves had always been cast in a negative light. Movies and stories stereotyped the wolf as a heartless killer, but Andrew knew they were inherently good. He pictured them rolling around on the ground playing with fellow wolf brothers. He knew they did eat some meat once in a while, but he remembered in the movie *Never Cry Wolf* that a wolf quite happily and successfully lived on mice. Mice, he thought, were pretty much expendable, being small and annoying and besides, they probably also ate berries and grass.

The hate-filled farmers had threatened to go on hunting parties and search for wolves. Since they couldn't kill them, they threatened to trap and release them far away. Andrew and his allies amended the law to prohibit the capture of wolves under any circumstances. The state would now protect the wolves and punish those who attempted to harm them.

Andrew and his colleagues also developed a public relations push to make people more comfortable with wolves. They produced nature documentaries explaining how the wolf was passive and harmless, with the focus being on how wolf mothers would raise and instruct their cubs. They sought to outlaw any hate speech or negative comments about wolves, but instead just made it taboo through a well-conceived public relations blitz.

The wolf observed the deer for a few minutes and then streaked away. Andrew was certain he ran off to play with his brothers.

"I knew it. Not dangerous at all."

Weeks had gone by since Andrew had seen the wolf, which Andrew had named Gray Protector in honor of his childhood companion. On one of his afternoon walks, he came across some tracks that troubled him. One was certainly a doe but the other was hard to make out. The creature had paws and claws, but its movements must have been quick because he couldn't make out a good track. He could determine with certainty the doe had been chased by some type of predator.

Incensed, Andrew followed the trail. It was easy to track since the animals were running at high speeds and making quick movements. He stopped short when he came upon drops of blood in the dirt. He knew the trail couldn't go much farther. The drops became more frequent and larger until he found the body of a deer.

His heart sank. Of all the animals in the valley, he hated finding dead deer the most. Such beautiful animals should never have to die. He was especially horrified that a deer would have to die such a brutal death. As he looked over the body, he noticed most of the flesh had been consumed and body parts had been scattered all over. Blood was everywhere and the deer's eyes remained wide open. The scene disturbed and saddened Andrew.

As he stared at the bloody doe his sadness turned to anger.

"What creature did this?" he asked.

Andrew examined the body for clues. It was clear that the predator was a hunter with sharp teeth and there were only a few animals in the area that fit that description; bears, cougars and – wolves. He shuddered.

"There's no way a wolf could take down a deer this size," he thought. "Wolves usually only go after small prey like rabbits and mice. There's no way Gray protector or any wolf could go after a doe."

He got down on his knees and looked over the wounds. He could see where teeth marks had ripped through the fur. His mind jumped to Evan who was always bullying the deer and certainly had the brawn to take out a deer.

"It *had* to be Evan!" Andrew said in disgust, as he looked for clues to further incriminate the bear. Close to the deer's spine Andrew found what he thought might be a claw mark. It looked suspiciously like Evan's huge, sharp claws."

He put his hand on the deer's fur, which was still

soft and slightly warm. Crouching down closer to inspect the chest cavity, he brushed aside pieces of gray fur to have a better look at the wounds. The bite marks appeared to be rather large, closely resembling Evan's large, pointy teeth."

The deer's head didn't appear to be damaged. The blackness of the eyes and the stillness of the deer's face haunted him. He felt a bond with the doe, like he had lost a friend. A sudden rush of anger overcame his feelings of sorrow.

"Evan will pay for this," he said softly to the doe. "I will avenge you!"

Glancing over the deer further he noticed something strange. Each of the legs from the knee down appeared to be in perfect shape except for the left hind leg, which was severely damaged just above the hoof. He looked closer and realized he could see all the way to the bone. The wound did not look fresh and the bone looked a bit dried out.

"That's an old wound," he said, a bit confused. "I wonder how she got -"

Andrew jumped backward and let out a scream as realization and shock took over him.

"It's her!" he said in a terrified voice.

He put his hands to his face and started sobbing as he fell to the ground. He turned away trying to process all the information. In the midst of his wailing he mumbled incoherently something about revenge and retribution. He rolled around on the ground for several minutes trying to collect his thoughts and control his emotions but his anger and sorrow couldn't be tamed. He gave into it.

After composing himself to some degree, he grabbed a nearby stick and began digging a grave. The dirt was soft but he had a hard time digging deep, which only increased his anger. He ferociously thrust the stick and lifted violently sending dirt in all directions while mumbling apologies to the doe mixed with threats against Evan.

Andrew had felt responsible for this doe's life since the day he saved her from the river. Every day since that moment he had taken pride in the fact that she was alive because of him.

As the pain and guilt overcame him, Andrew began to realize he wasn't to blame; it was Evan who did this out of pure hatred and intolerance. He didn't understand why Evan would do this, as bears didn't typically eat deer and why Evan would pick out this doe in particular. It seemed personal.

"This must have been some sort of vengeance kill to get back at me for throwing rocks at him or to reassert his dominance," Andrew reasoned.

Andrew gently slid the body into the hole and started covering it with dirt. When he was nearly finished covering the body he threw down his stick and walked away with a heavy heart. He vowed never to return to that spot again but also to never forget what had happened there.

## Chapter 12: The Big Bang

Andrew's sorrow stayed with him for many days. The only way to forget about the pain was to stay actively engaged in the workings of the valley. As time went by, the pain subsided and Andrew allowed himself to relax.

He spent most of his early evenings exploring and checking on his work. Late summer nights were the perfect time to make a fire and sit back in a chair and ponder. He couldn't help but think about life back home and wonder what was going on there. Usually, however, he would think about his work and how satisfied he was to be helping the valley survive.

One warm summer night, Andrew lay on the ground looking up at the stars and moon. He could hear the trickle of the nearby river as the stars glistened beautifully above him. He thought of the creation and the brilliance that took place when the earth and the stars and planets came to be. He reflected on the balance in the natural world. He marveled that with his help everything could work so perfectly and fairly around him. The animals instinctively went about their business while the trees grew toward the light of the sun. The water fell from the sky and then flowed back to the sea. Each spring all was renewed.

His heart seemed to swell as he took in the beauty around him and contemplated the massive scale of the cosmos above him. All the animals, the plants, the water, the rocks, the lights and the planets themselves testified of the beginning and ultimate creation.

Two tears emerged in his eyes as he looked up and meditated. He was overwhelmed by the emotion he felt, not prepared for the tears that now slid down his cheeks onto the back of his neck. He rarely cried but this scene was so awe-inspiring that it was difficult to keep his emotions in check.

As he lay on the ground gazing up at the sky, he felt closer to the Big Bang than ever before. Andrew had studied it in high school and college and had seen a few documentaries about it, but until he got away from the bright lights of the city and away from the pressures of society, he never really appreciated it. Now that his mind was truly prepared, he felt a connection.

It seemed to speak to him of beginnings. It opened

his eyes to the possibilities of millions of particles bonding together to form the earth. He thought of the young earth in its molten stage, burning hot and swirling with magma. He imagined the first molecules and how they had sprung into everything he saw before him now.

"It all makes perfect sense!"

He knew he was part of that creation and the universe had a plan for him and that he was supposed to be in the valley. Everything around him pointed to that magical time when all things started from one molecule.

As Andrew gazed out at the countless stars and beautiful celestial lights, he realized he was truly content. He drifted off to sleep knowing that he was an important part of the Big Bang's course.

## Chapter 13: The Duel

*Antlers hardened as autumn approached. Mating season was coming and the pecking order had yet to be determined. The bucks knew the time was at hand that they would compete for mating rights.*

*Dominance was at stake with the prevailing buck earning the right to pass his genes to the next generation. Only the strongest buck would assure future offspring the greatest chance of survival. The losing buck would have another chance to take the head of the herd, but it would have to wait. The endurance of the herd was at stake.*

Andrew awakened one morning to a strange noise. It sounded like two sticks bring banged together. The noise recurred about every thirty seconds. Andrew laughed as he thought of a movie he had seen many years before where someone banged sticks together to frighten mountain lions.

Dressing quickly, he left his tent to investigate. He didn't go far before he could see two bucks with antlers locked together. The bucks were pushing and pulling each other while a few does looked on. They would lean back on their hind legs and then crash into each other, unlock and crash together again.

Andrew was mesmerized by the raw power of the animals. He hadn't seen many bucks since arriving in the valley and always felt lucky when he saw one. Now, seeing two together was a real treat.

The bucks continued attacking one another – unaware that Andrew was watching. After witnessing the duel for a few minutes, Andrew became concerned the bucks were being too violent. Andrew hated war because he believed it was all about power and dominance. War always resulted in establishing a winner and a loser. Countries, like people and animals, should learn to get along.

Andrew also worried about the affect the bucks' fighting would have on the does and the younger deer. The younger bucks witnessing the fighting would learn to grow up and become fighters themselves. Even if this was something bucks had done for generations, it was a foolish tradition that was being perpetuated unnecessarily.

Seeing an opportunity to change the negative traditions of these bucks, he rushed toward them like a parent trying to break up a fight between siblings.

"Stop! Don't fight!" he shouted as loudly as he could while waving his arms hoping that the yelling would at least scare them into solving their differences another way. "There's no need to fight. You can work it out. You're both winners."

The bucks unlocked antlers and backed away from Andrew slowly. They seemed confused. Andrew continued walking toward them.

"Don't fight! This is stupid!"

As Andrew continued his approach, the two bucks and the does bolted away from him. They leaped over logs and dodged trees as they fled.

"Mission accomplished! I'm glad I put a stop to that. They could have been really hurt. Those bucks need to learn life is not always about establishing dominance. Hopefully they have learned the better way."

Andrew went about his usual business of checking on his projects and recording temperatures when he heard antlers crashing again. He dropped what he was doing and ran to the noise.

He saw what appeared to be the same bucks fighting in the same manner as before. Without taking the time to admire their strength, Andrew ran toward them waving his arms and yelling.

The bucks fled again along with a few does. Andrew felt agitated they hadn't learned the lesson.

He was determined to train them to resolve their problems peacefully. Every time he heard the antlers crashing, he would rush to them to break up the fight. He sought to find some way to communicate how to share.

"They've got to learn to be peaceful. Fighting never helps the situation."

Over the next few weeks, Andrew rushed to break up the bucks over fifteen times. Each time the bucks would unlock their antlers, look at Andrew for a second and then flee into the trees.

On one such occasion, Andrew was running towards the sound of the bucks locking antlers and saw a curious sight. Just as he was arriving to break up the activity, he saw the bucks stop and look around. The does too became nervous and fled quickly. Andrew caught a glimpse of Grey Protector slinking along the edge of the tree line. The wolf had broken up the fighting. Andrew was thrilled to have help in disrupting the violence in the valley and was grateful for the assistance.

Eventually, the fighting grew more infrequent until it stopped completely.

Andrew was certain he had convinced the bucks to resolve their conflict without resorting to violence. It seemed to him that if nature gave out peace prizes, then he would have been nominated for stopping violence and encouraging productive dialogue. Grey

Protector also deserved recognition as a trusted ally.

"That deer family will never be the same now. They are on a new, better path from here on out."

Andrew decided to reward them by providing even larger rations of food and water each day. He also decided to reward himself with an honorary Nobel Peace Prize.

# Chapter 14: The Salmon

*Gliding through ocean water, the salmon sensed something that had been there since birth. It was as natural as life itself. The feeling was more than just premonition; it was revelation. It was the salmon's purpose. To deny this urge would be to deny its very existence.*

*Instinctively it knew the path ahead would be dangerous and difficult, but felt a powerful yearning to answer the call regardless of the obstacles it would encounter. The obstacles, it knew, would weed out the weak ones. It knew the journey would be its last, but all that mattered was that it was going home.*

Summer turned to fall rather quickly in the valley. With September came cooler weather, colorful leaves and shorter days. The animals seemed more anxious and frantic – making last-minute preparations for the coming winter.

Andrew's anger about the doe's death resurfaced over the days and weeks that followed. He began carrying his rifle on walks and started deviating from his usual path in the hope he might encounter Evan. He hadn't resolved what he would do when he saw Evan, but wanted to be prepared.

Andrew desperately wanted to find out where Evan lived so he could monitor him closely. He thought it odd that he had only seen him one day though he believed Evan didn't live too far from the valley. This made him wonder if the bear was around more often but was able to avoid Andrew.

Anytime he went for a walk he would scan the ground specifically for bear tracks. Everywhere he went he kept his eyes open for signs of Evan.

On one of his hunting expeditions, he was walking along the bank when a splash startled him near the shore. As he looked toward the splash he saw something dart upstream. The thing was about three feet long and seemed too big to have been a fish. Suddenly, he saw two more dark shapes flash upstream.

"Those were definitely fish, but they were so big. Where did they come from?" He looked closely for a few minutes and saw more large fish sailing past him in the river; all of them headed upstream.

"Those are salmon!"

Andrew looked closely at the river and noticed a dozen salmon working their way upstream. He recalled September was Salmon Days in the little town in which he grew up. It was a fun little event that corresponded with the salmon going up river to spawn.

This was about that time of year but he was surprised that salmon made it this far up the river, thinking they would have spawned much lower. Having accepted the fact that spawning salmon were heading up this high he was surprised that there weren't more of them. As a kid, he remembered thousands of salmon heading up river to spawn. Andrew had a vivid memory of standing on a bridge and it seemed like he couldn't even see the riverbed because there were so many salmon.

"Why are there so few coming up the river? There should be more than this."

In order to investigate, he broke from his usual hiking schedule to walk downstream along the bank of the river. Every minute or two a small group of salmon would dart upstream. He came to an open area with a small waterfall. Unable to see the bottom, he approached eagerly to see how big it was.

At the top of the waterfall, Andrew peered over the edge looking for more salmon. Looking up at him only about fifteen feet away were the dark eyes of a huge bear. Andrew stopped midstride and screamed.

The scream momentarily startled Evan who bolted off to the opposite bank, then turned to look at Andrew, who was standing still as a statue.

Andrew thought about drawing his gun, but wasn't sure he would be fast enough. All the feeling he had while digging the doe's grave resurfaced in his mind. As his anger and resolve began to grow, Evan made the first move.

Evan, upon seeing Andrew, walked directly and purposely back into the river and resumed his position just below the waterfall. This upset Andrew even more.

"Isn't he afraid of me? Doesn't he respect my territory at all?"

Andrew watched as Evan stood in the river waiting for something. He seemed preoccupied with the water. The waterfall was about four feet high and Evan was standing on some rocks so his head was right in the middle of it.

"He's probably just grandstanding; trying to intimidate me. That's the only thing bullies know how to do."

Just then a large salmon shot out from the pool below directly into the waterfall. Evan snapped at it but missed, the salmon fell into the waterfall and back down into the pool. Another salmon flew past Evan's snapping jaws but failed to make it up the waterfall. Seconds later two more salmon leapt out of the water but failed to clear the waterfall.

The next salmon shot out of the water and directly into Evan's open jaws. Evan clinched his teeth around the helpless salmon, which was flopping its head and tail trying to get free from Evan's grasp. Evan tilted his head up, opened his mouth for a split second and then clinched his teeth even harder on the salmon. This dealt a serious blow to the salmon whose pink flesh was now exposed and whose squirming ceased completely. Evan, clinching his trophy tightly, moved toward Andrew.

Andrew didn't know whether to back up or hold his ground, but Evan didn't seem to care what he did. Preoccupied with his catch, he proudly dropped it on the bank about fifteen feet from where Andrew was standing. He looked at Andrew for a split second and then began ripping the flesh of the salmon while holding it down with its paw. Convinced that Evan was no threat to him at the moment, Andrew watched as more salmon attempted to clear the waterfall on their way to their spawning beds. For every fifty attempts, only a few salmon made it to the upper river.

Andrew now understood why there were so few salmon upriver. These two obstacles – Evan and the waterfall – stood between the salmon and their spawning beds. It pained Andrew to see the salmon exert such energy and effort only to fail and fall back into the pool. He wondered what the salmon could do to increase their chances, feeling it was every salmon's right to spawn.

As Andrew analyzed the situation, Evan finished devouring his salmon and went straight back into the river to get another. In thirty minutes Andrew watched, Evan snag three salmon and only four salmon made it to the upper river.

"This isn't fair. These salmon are working hard and doing their best. This waterfall is too high and Evan is just greedy."

Andrew couldn't stand to watch as more salmon struggled and failed and being around Evan was really annoying him. He turned around and walked up the river, but the pain of the salmons' struggle stayed with him. Upon reaching camp, he was still troubled.

"They can't make it up that waterfall; it's too high for them. It's ridiculous. They can't be expected to jump that high. And to have to jump it with some stupid bear waiting there for a free lunch is impossible. I have to do something."

Andrew spent the evening concocting a plan to help the salmon. His goal was to make it possible for every single salmon to reach the spawning beds.

"They need to spawn," he said. "They have a right to spawn and I have a duty to help them."

Early the next morning Andrew eagerly walked downstream to the waterfall. Wearing his old waders, he held his rifle in front of him in case he saw Evan again. As he arrived he saw the salmon still struggling. Evan was nowhere in sight. He walked downstream to get a good view of the falls.

Andrew noticed that most of the water was coming down the center where the salmon were jumping. The distance from the pool to the top of the waterfall was about four feet. On the left side Andrew noticed a dry bed of rocks where it appeared the water had flowed during spring runoff. There would be no obstacles for the salmon if the water were flowing through that channel and they could easily slip their way up river.

Of course, if the salmon traveled that simpler pathway it would make it easier for Evan to catch them. But, judging by Evan's success rate at the waterfall Andrew did not think it would be a big problem.

"If it *is* a problem, I will solve it."

Andrew waded across the river below the waterfall and traversed the bank on the opposite side to the dry riverbed. He began at the bottom of the rock bed and started moving rocks to make a wider channel right in the middle. After an hour he had a channel that was nearly a foot and a half deep, four feet wide and about ten feet long. The channel was enough for three or four salmon to ascend at the same time.

# LIBERAL IN NATURE

With the channel dug out, it was ready to receive water. At the top of the waterfall Andrew began moving rocks around until a small trickle started to go down the channel. He knew he had to raise the water level above the waterfall and lower the entrance to the channel at the same time. He decided to plug up the middle part of the waterfall so the water would spread out to the sides and would fill the channel with enough flowing water for the salmon to ascend.

It was not an easy job to plug up the hole. It took Andrew several hours before he noticed any difference in water flow. However, after moving a few key rocks, the flow to the middle of the waterfall slowed noticeably and the water coming down the river spread out to the banks.

The salmon swam frantically in the pool below. Uncertain about the creature in the middle of the waterfall, they bumped into each other and crashed into rocks.

Andrew waded to the side where he'd made his channel and saw that water was now flowing freely over the top of the riverbed and down through his channel. He had formed his own tiny stream in a matter of five hours.

Concluding that the channel was big enough for the salmon, he waited to watch them swim through. Andrew watched for five minutes and none of the salmon took advantage of the new stream.

"They realize the channel is there. They must not know it can lead them safely to their spawning beds."

Salmon were still attempting to jump the waterfall, which was now a more difficult and precarious feat since the waterfall wasn't receiving as much water.

"I guess I'm going to have to lead them to it. They are beautiful fish, but must not be very bright. They don't know what's good for them."

Andrew hiked down below the waterfall and waded across the river again to the other side. He felt like he was herding cattle as he entered the water and began splashing in an attempt to drive the salmon toward the channel. He passed through the pool below the waterfall and made it to the channel and still no salmon attempted to ascend the channel.

Frustrated, Andrew got out of the river and walked down stream about fifty yards. He got back into the water and waded upstream in an effort to get them to go up the channel. This time it worked.

The first salmon appeared to be looking for any way to escape and seeing the water flowing into the pool from the channel it darted straight up into the upper river. Soon another salmon made the ascent. Then, another salmon made it and then another. The remaining fish, seeing their fleeing peers, followed suit and swam for safety. The channel was now churning with salmon.

## LIBERAL IN NATURE

Andrew felt like a genius. He watched as the salmon all filed through the channel to safety. He smiled to know that he had saved them all. They were making it home because of him.

Andrew walked to the edge of the channel to see the salmon up close. He could reach out and touch them, if he wanted. Some had dark spots forming but most still looked healthy with their shiny red and silver scales. Salmon happened to be one of Andrew's favorite foods ever since he had gone salmon fishing in Canada as a boy. He realized he hadn't had it for a long time.

The main source of protein in Andrew's diet since coming to the valley was trout and nuts. He had grown tired of trout and thought he might enjoy salmon for a change. He had saved so many salmon; he should be entitled to reserve a few for himself. He grew excited at the thought of cooking a large slab of salmon over a fire.

Hordes of salmon were still darting up the channel. Andrew stepped into the water causing them to adjust and swim around him. He stood in the middle of the channel and bent down with his hands in the water. As a salmon attempted to swim by, he quickly moved his hands forward and shoveled it toward the shore.

The salmon flew through the air and landed hard on the rocks. It flopped furiously trying to get back to water. Andrew was surprised that he had so easily caught it. He scurried over and knelt down while the salmon continued to flop intensely. Andrew grabbed a medium-sized rock and dealt a few quick blows to its head. He washed his hands in the river and returned to the channel to catch another.

Within ten minutes, Andrew was walking back to camp with three large salmon. He carried them by their gills like trophies. He thought of them, not as trophies of the hunt, but as recompense for his work to save their fellow salmon. He didn't like killing them, but knew that if he didn't get enough protein and strength, his work in the valley would be diminished and then all the animals would suffer.

Andrew filleted one salmon and cooked one of the slabs. He left the other two on a rope tied to a tree, and let them soak in the cool river to stay fresh. It was wonderful to have a different taste than the usual trout. He felt the salmon's strength go into him. He decided to cook the other slab the next day and then dry the remaining salmon. He went to bed feeling strong and healthy.

The next morning, Andrew awoke to an unfamiliar sound of grunting and sniffing outside his tent. He sat up, listened intently and instantly knew some creature was in his camp. Unzipping the door a crack, he saw Evan chewing on the slab he had saved. His makeshift table was tipped over and utensils were scattered in the dirt. Evan didn't notice Andrew but kept tearing into the salmon flesh with his teeth.

Andrew couldn't believe the bear was only ten feet away from him. All of his searching had been useless and yet, here was the bear in his camp. Andrew didn't know what to do. He was still in shock and a little frightened from waking up to such a scene. He grabbed his rifle and went back to the door. Evan had just finished the salmon and started sniffing around camp.

Unzipping the tent door quietly, he stuck the rifle barrel out of the small opening and pulled the trigger. Andrew fell back into his tent as Evan leaped in surprise and bolted away knocking down everything in his path.

As he lay in shock on the tent floor looking up, he saw Rob flying overhead. He thought Rob was coming to make sure he was okay, but instead flew straight for the opening in the door. Andrew didn't have time to zip the door shut before Rob flew through the opening and out into the blue sky.

Andrew jumped to his feet and hurried outside but there was no sign of Rob.

"Rob!" he yelled desperately. "Rob! Come back!"

Andrew crumpled to the ground. His only friend and companion had gone. In an instance of confusion and ignorance, Rob had flown away.

"The gun shot must have frightened and

disoriented him. And the gun shot, of course, was Evan's fault," Andrew concluded as he looked at the mess outside his tent. "That bear is going to suffer."

Every few days Andrew went to the waterfall to see if salmon were still swimming up the channel he built for them. Each day he was proud to see salmon filing through it on their way to their spawning beds. Andrew would watch them for a few minutes and then would catch one for dinner.

A week after Rob flew away, Andrew went to the waterfall and saw Evan standing in the middle of the channel. Andrew could see two salmon carcasses spread out over the rocks.

"That greedy bully! He can't ever get enough."

Tired of Evan's greed, he was ready to get revenge.

"Hey Evan!" he yelled, cupping his hands together, hoping to scare him off. "Let them spawn! Leave them alone!"

Evan ignored Andrew's calls. Just as Andrew was going to yell again, Evan reached his paw into the water and pulled out a salmon. He immediately sank his teeth through the spine. The salmon flopped back and forth but it was too late.

Evan stepped onto the rocks where he began devouring the salmon as he had done with the previous two victims.

Andrew walked quietly to the bank of the river

and knelt down on one knee. He took his rifle off his shoulder and aimed the rifle at Evan's heart.

"I have him in my sights and I can make the valley a better place just by pulling this trigger. His greed and arrogance have gone too far. He doesn't care about other animals. He's a bully."

Andrew was about to pull the trigger but decided he needed further evidence of Evan's atrocities before he could kill him. Instead, Andrew aimed at Evan's paw, which was holding the salmon as he pulled the flesh off with his teeth.

Andrew squeezed the trigger and shot a bullet clean through Evan's left palm. Evan jumped back and groaned. Staggering to his feet, he took off in a frenzied limp.

"Not bad. That will level the playing field a bit. He won't be able to catch as many fish or deer with *that* wound."

Andrew crossed the river to look at the remains of the salmon Evan had greedily killed. Observing little white bones scattered all over the rocks with skin and blood, he noticed something intriguing; a bloody footprint.

"He's bleeding and walking and will leave a trail leading right to his den."

After tracking Evan for an hour, Andrew finally saw where the bloody trail lead. He stood fifty yards from a large rock wall with an opening right in the middle.

"He's probably had enough for today," Andrew thought. "But now I know where he lives, I can pay him a visit as needed."

# Chapter 15: The Squirrels

*The squirrel knows winter is coming. It feels it in the atmosphere and sees it in the colors of the valley. It knows there is no time to wait. There will be no one to feed it when the snow comes. It must rely on its thrift and hard work. It instinctively knows how much to store. It knows what it will take to make it through. Fatigue must be ignored. Pain cannot exist. The squirrel has one job; survive the winter.*

Autumn settled into the valley. Bright red, yellow and orange leaves interspersed with the evergreen trees on the mountainside. The atmosphere was changing and the animals seemed to know what it meant. They acted differently, seeming more earnest in their movements. The beautiful leaves were falling from the trees. Some things seemed to slow down, as all of the creatures instinctively knew winter was coming.

Andrew noticed behavioral changes particularly among the squirrels. Normally, they frolicked and played casually, but now they seemed focused. Most of them seemed to be frantically searching for food to store.

A few of the squirrels hung out around Andrew's camp. They sometimes wandered in to eat crumbs left behind. Other times they just observed as he chopped wood or worked on a project. Now *he* was the one interested in watching *them*.

There were two squirrels in which he took particular interest. The first would scamper up a tree with a nut in its mouth, deposit it inside the tree and then scurry away to find more. It seemed incredibly anxious about something, almost to the point of paranoia. It seemed quite protective and territorial.

The other squirrel didn't seem to be searching for nuts at all. It was sitting idly on a tree branch with very little interest in the other squirrel's efforts. Andrew tried to figure out what he was doing and why he wasn't looking for nuts. The second squirrel looked lethargic and was notably thinner than the first squirrel, appearing confused and disoriented. Andrew didn't know what the problem was, but knew it would have more serious problems with no nuts to store against the winter.

"That guy better start gathering nuts before the

snow comes, or he's not going to make it through the winter," Andrew thought.

At that moment, Andrew saw the busy, fat squirrel carrying two nuts in its mouth. It was probably twice the size of the thin squirrel with a large stomach that rubbed against the ground when it walked. The fat squirrel buried one nut at the base of a tree on the east side of camp and the other inside a hole in the tree. The squirrel hurriedly ran back down the tree and disappeared for a moment only to return a minute later with two more nuts.

The fat squirrel then went to a different tree and buried the nuts in separate holes inside that tree, disappearing several more times and returning with nuts to bury in different locations. Andrew counted at least ten different stashes where the squirrel buried nuts.

The fat squirrel's incredible display of efficiency and thrift impressed Andrew. Despite its large size, it moved with quickness and agility bounding up and down trees and over bushes. It worked relentlessly. Each time before hiding a nut, it would bite into the shell, lick the inside and then bury the nut. It looked like meticulous work but the fat squirrel did it with incredible focus and determination. Despite his admiration for the fat squirrel, Andrew couldn't shake the image of the thin squirrel sitting on its branch, not gathering food for the winter.

His appreciation for the fat squirrel's efficiency began to wane as he realized that the it was depriving the thin squirrel of nuts. The reason the thin squirrel wasn't getting nuts was because the fat squirrel had pushed him out of the market, making it impossible for the thin squirrel to make it. It wasn't the thin squirrel's fault. He was the victim, as there was no way for him to compete with that fatty.

"This isn't fair," Andrew mumbled to himself.

Andrew waited for the fat squirrel to scamper off and then quickly ran over to one of its stashes in the ground and dug it up until he got to the nuts. Placing a handful of nuts in his bag, he moved on to the next stash where he did the same thing. The fat squirrel was in his main nest so he was unaware of Andrew's thieving. Andrew cleaned out four more of the fat squirrel's stashes.

At the last two stashes, Andrew put the nuts in his own pocket, thinking that winter might be rough for him too and the nuts would be a change from his usual fare.

Andrew had brought a couple of cans of mixed nuts with him, but he didn't like the Brazil nuts that were included.

"Maybe these nuts are better."

With a bag full of nuts, Andrew approached the thin squirrel's nest slowly as not to scare it. Hearing approaching footsteps, the thin squirrel mustered the

## LIBERAL IN NATURE

strength to climb out of the nest and crawl to the other side of the tree and watch as Andrew emptied all of the nuts into its nest.

"Now he won't have to gather nuts and he won't have to go crawling around looking for hidden stashes. He will have all the nuts he needs right there in his nest."

As he walked back to his camp, Andrew noticed the fat squirrel standing on hind legs staring at him nervously. He stood motionless, waiting for Andrew to turn his back or look away so he could run to his nest. The fat squirrel had no idea what had happened to his supplies. Andrew looked at him unsympathetically.

"You've still got plenty of nuts and you've got plenty of fat to live on for the winter," he said out loud. "There is no way you could possibly eat all of those nuts in one winter. It's better when you spread the nuts around. Share the wealth, buddy."

Back at camp, Andrew sat down by the fire and reflected on the good deed he had done. He hoped that maybe he had earned some goodwill with the thin squirrel. Helping less fortunate animals and plants had become quite fulfilling for him.

"I am getting better at finding opportunities to save these animals. This may have been my greatest accomplishment yet."

The thin squirrel most likely would not have

survived the winter without him. He imagined that if he ever needed help, the thin squirrel would remember what Andrew had done and would help him. Of course, the thin squirrel could probably never save *his* life so he wasn't likely to repay him in full, but perhaps he could spread the word to the other squirrels that he was friendly and there was nothing to fear. Or maybe they could become friends now that Rob was gone. The thin squirrel might provide some companionship and entertainment Andrew had been missing since Rob's tragic departure.

The thought of entertainment randomly made Andrew think about a waterskiing squirrel he once saw at a boat show. As a kid he had been thoroughly entertained by such a ridiculous little squirrel riding around on tiny skis behind a remote controlled boat. It was many years later Andrew realized the animal cruelty in that display.

The seemingly innocent act of teaching a squirrel to water-ski had captured his young mind, but once enlightened, Andrew was disgusted by how easily he had been duped. This lead him to join PETA and lobby for them in Washington D.C. He had spent many hours demonstrating and protesting against organizations he deemed harmful to animals.

The help he rendered to the thin squirrel must have been a subconscious attempt to repair the damage that humans did to its squirrel relative - the water-skier. Andrew hoped that wherever the waterskiing squirrel was, he had found peace, as had many college mascots Andrew had helped throughout the years.

# Chapter 16: The Solution

Andrew couldn't believe how fast the time seemed to be going by. Autumn was already beginning to turn into winter. The days were getting shorter and colder and the valley seemed to be slowing down. Having already survived a winter in the valley, Andrew was determined to be more active this time around. He would slow down his operations but wouldn't stay in his tent as much as the previous winter. Just before Andrew expected the cold to really set in, the valley suddenly warmed up for a week. Temperatures rose and the all-day sunshine made it feel like spring.

"Global warming," he thought with excitement.

Weeks had passed since Andrew saved the spawning salmon and he was realizing there were consequences to saving all of them. The salmon had traveled up the river to spawn and die but then their carcasses floated down into the lake where they remained to decompose. With the sudden warm weather, the valley began to stink so much that it was making Andrew sick.

The river was filled with rotting salmon carcasses. Some of them were washed down the river, but many also washed ashore. Andrew couldn't stand living so close to the horrible stench.

Though he did not regret saving the salmon, he was becoming more and more annoyed at the stench of the valley. While thinking about what to do with his new problem, he realized there would be other unintended consequences that would adversely affect him. Because so many salmon reached their spawning beds, there would be an overabundance of salmon eggs and salmon babies. He estimated that, based on the success rate of the salmon trying to get over the waterfall before he made the channel, twenty times more salmon had spawned this year than would have otherwise.

Twenty times the amount of spawning salmon most likely meant twenty times the amount of baby salmon being born. He wondered if it were good to have so many baby salmon swimming around the river and lake. He worried that they might overpopulate the habitat. He wasn't sure what they ate but wondered if it might be a limited resource.

"If only there were a way to allow the salmon to

spawn while still not overburdening the river. It's every salmon's right to make it up the river and to spawn in safety. However, it is the river's right to have balance and I must also ensure that I give the river *its* right."

After thinking through the problem most of the day, he decided to go to the river for inspiration. Though the stench of the decomposing fish was stronger by the river, Andrew knew he needed the river's help. He put on his waders, grabbed his fishing rod and walked to a fishing hole just below the lake.

As he stepped off the bank into the river, he remembered something he had seen many times while fishing in public waters back in society. There were sometimes signs on the banks of rivers warning fisherman not to walk through spawning beds because it would damage the fish population. Andrew was always respectful of the signs because he wanted to protect the fish.

The memory sparked an idea of how he could accomplish both of his goals of promoting free spawning rights and protecting the overall good of the river.

Leaving his fishing rod on the bank of the river, he spent the rest of the day tromping through spawning beds trying to step on as many salmon eggs as possible. As he walked, he dragged his boots on the riverbed hoping to overturn rocks that might be protecting eggs.

He walked up and down the river in a systematic manner. He would start close to the bank and follow its natural curve upstream to a certain point. Upon reaching that point, he would turn around, take a step toward the middle of the river and walk back downstream.

As he walked through the spawning beds he started seeing lumps of salmon eggs floating downstream. He was encouraged by what he saw. His plan was working. Every bit of floating roe was a victory and he would wade out even farther.

Andrew felt badly for the salmon who had worked so hard to spawn the eggs, but he reminded himself that they were dead and they had died happy and fulfilled. Besides, they were stinking up the valley so he wasn't overly concerned for them. They got what they were entitled to, but he also knew he had to intercede or else the whole river ecosystem would get out of whack.

Andrew spent the next few weeks walking through spawning beds for miles of river. Each time he saw a batch of salmon eggs floating down the river he smiled because he knew he was properly regulating the environment and the population. He also realized that trout downstream would be getting fat on those eggs, which would also benefit him when he caught those trout. He started grabbing the eggs that he saw so he could use them as bait for fishing during the winter.

"The trout won't be able to pass up some bright, juicy salmon eggs when food is scarce."

Andrew wondered if he should leave sections of spawning beds untouched. After all, if he took out *all* of the eggs, no baby salmon would be born in the spring. That would be disastrous. He concluded that even if he tried to terminate all the eggs, he would ultimately miss more than he'd find, which would probably leave a healthy population of baby salmon. But, if he left some sections untouched, there would most likely be overpopulation.

So Andrew decided to walk through every spawning bed confident that his margin of error would produce the right number of salmon offspring. After completing his procedure, he had a full supply of salmon eggs for fishing, everything seemed back in harmony and he had done an incredible service to the valley once again.

"*All* the salmon get to spawn at will, the river stays in balance, and I get bait for catching trout. It's a win-win-win," he said joyfully. "The *only* negative in the whole plan is that the valley still stinks. There isn't much I can do about that and it should go away soon so I guess I will just have to tough it out."

Andrew was pleased with his quick and brilliant response to a potential disaster. He felt like he had closed out the year on a high note and he was now ready to slow it down his efforts and take a break for the winter.

# Chapter 17: The Winter

Winter had firmly set in earlier than the previous year and, though Andrew was sad that his activities in the valley would slow down, he knew he could use a break. He felt bad about not providing food and water for the deer anymore, but thought they would probably be fine. The deer gathered together near his camp each day, waiting for him to put food out.

"They've survived winters before," he said to comfort himself. "They can make it."

Andrew did not intend to stay dormant during the winter. He had been waiting patiently for winter so he could make his way back to Evan's den and get revenge for all he had done to Andrew and the animals throughout the summer and fall.

After waiting a few more weeks to make sure Evan was hibernating, Andrew hiked to the den. Everything looked different with snow covering, but after some effort searching the mountainside he managed to find the entrance. Entering the cave cautiously, Andrew strapped his rifle over his shoulder while holding a knife in one hand and a flashlight in the other hand. He crawled forward slowly with his heart beating loud enough he was afraid Evan might hear it. The cave wasn't as deep as he expected and having crawled to the end of it, Andrew realized the slumbering giant was directly in front of him.

Evan lay still but Andrew could see that he continued breathing slowly. Paranoia set in as Andrew wondered what Evan would do to him if he woke up and found him in the cave. He thought of how big Evan had looked standing on his hind legs in the water, but Andrew convinced himself that the bear was in a deep sleep and would not sense his presence. He forcefully shoved his fears into the back of his mind. Wasting no time, he knelt down in front of the bear with his knife in his right hand. Andrew placed the knife on the ground by the bear's throat and hastily retrieved his Leatherman from his pocket while extending the wire cutters. He put the flashlight in his mouth and held it tightly with his teeth.

Andrew quickly, without thinking about what the bear could do to him, grabbed one of Evan's giant paws with his left hand and with his right hand held the wire cutters right up to the claws. His hands were shaking uncontrollably as he held the clippers up to

Evan's claws. Andrew took a few deep breaths and then, one by one, he clipped off half an inch of each claw so there was hardly even a nail protruding from the fur. Evan's massive body rumbled midway through the third claw. Andrew jumped backwards against the cave wall, ready to run for his life. After waiting in the darkness for what was actually about sixty seconds, but seemed much longer, he continued with the remaining claws.

Andrew gently grabbed the other paw and Evan let out a groan. Andrew jumped back again, his heart racing. After waiting a minute, he grabbed the paw again and noticed the bullet hole through Evan's palm.

"Not a bad shot," Andrew thought as he admired his marksmanship.

Careful not to disturb the wound, Andrew carefully clipped each of the remaining claws. When he was finished clipping the wounded paw, he then clipped the claws of the bear's hind legs.

"Good luck holding salmon with no claws," he whispered. "Have fun clawing trees with those stubs. You're lucky I don't have a tooth polisher, cause I'd take care of those sharp teeth too."

Andrew stood up to look over the sleeping bear, feeling much more emboldened now. Despite the fear and adrenaline coursing through his body, he enjoyed knowing that if desired, he could end Evan's life right then. His restraint showed he was morally superior, because Evan surely would not have done the same for him. He wanted to let Evan know he had been in Andrew's hands and that Andrew had chosen to deliver him.

Keeping a tight grip on his rifle, he walked around the cave rubbing his clothes on all the walls to leave his scent for the bear. He had a half-eaten granola bar in his backpack, which he strategically left by the bear's nose as a sign. When he finished, he still had the overwhelming feeling of revenge. He wanted to do more.

"The bully is helpless in front of me. What can I do to get the ultimate revenge?" Andrew thought, struggling to find the right symbolic gesture.

Andrew remembered that day in gym class in the showers when the bully had humiliated the seventh grader by urinating on him across the shower. The thought of it disturbed him. He hated thinking about it.

Andrew's anger grew. He wanted to pay the bear back for all the horrible and humiliating things bullies had ever done to him or anyone else. He wanted the revenge to be just as humiliating and demoralizing. He wanted the bear to feel small and helpless.

"You need to know what it's like."

Andrew took the rifle off his shoulder, cocked it and pointed it at the bear's heart. He stepped closer until he was standing directly over the helpless bear. Then he unzipped his pants and started urinating on Evan's body. True jubilation overtook Andrew as he pondered and marveled at the brilliance of this gesture.

The free-flowing urine splashing on the bear's fur not only represented payback to the bear and to all bullies; it was also the ultimate signal to the bear that Andrew had been in his cave and marked his territory. It was the ultimate warning to Evan that his life was in Andrew's hands and he could take it away at any time.

"I have marked you now," Andrew whispered. "You are mine. I own you. You better watch what you do or next time you'll have bullets coming at you instead of my piss. Enjoy the rest of winter."

Andrew zipped up his pants and began crawling back out of the cave. He looked back at the bear one last time before leaving. He had once looked so tough and intimidating, but now it looked weak and pathetic. Once he had seemed to be coated with power and now he was coated with urine. Once he had pulled salmon apart with its razor-sharp claws and now his claws looked like snails barely peaking out of their shells.

As Andrew left the cave he thought of that little seventh grader who all those years before had been humiliated in the shower. He wished he knew the boy's name and where he lived to relieve him of all his suffering and tell him that he got even with the bully and settled the score by urinating on a hibernating bear in a cave in the mountains.

"He's in my debt now," Andrew thought. "The score is settled."

# Chapter 18: The Snow

The winter was going much better than the previous one had. Ever since Andrew had managed to get revenge against Evan, he had felt upbeat and chipper. The short winter had already been a complete success in his mind.

The Deer still gathered each day around his camp, but he didn't know what to do for them. He tried boiling water and leaving it out for them, but they wouldn't drink it when it was hot and it would freeze too fast for them to enjoy it when it was cold.

"I've done all I can for you," he told them. "Go find your own food now, but don't forget what I've done for you."

As the weeks went by, their numbers dwindled and Andrew assumed they had found food elsewhere.

He spent most of his time in the tent; leaving a few times a day to make his usual records, do a bit of exploring and fishing. The salmon roe proved to be the perfect bait for catching trout in the winter. He hardly had to leave his line in the water for a few seconds before he had a bite.

One cold winter morning Andrew awoke to a new layer of snow. The winter had been fairly mild with only about a foot of snow. In one night, the storm had doubled that amount.

Gazing out of his tent window, he loved how the fresh snow made the valley so quiet and peaceful. The glistening white world around him seemed like a new planet on an alternate universe.

On this morning, as he gazed over the landscape, Andrew paid special attention to the trees. He noticed the tall tree near his camp, in particular, was weighed down heavily by snow resting on its branches. It looked much older now than it had the previous spring. He thought it must be a thousand years old and it pained him to think that the recent snowfall might bring it down. Its branches seemed to scream out at him to relieve them of the weight and pressure they were under.

"He must be glad I cut all those branches off last spring or else he would really be weighed down," Andrew thought while proudly remembering how he had provided sunlight for the smaller trees. Deeply concerned, he compared the burden of each of the trees. Although the smaller trees also looked weighed down with snow, they were not quite as burdened as the tall tree.

Andrew had always felt somewhat of a brotherhood with trees. When he was in elementary school and first learned about global deforestation, he felt horrible. He was glad when his teacher started passing out recycled paper to the class, even though he hated its grayish tint and rough texture.

As a kid he looked for ways to help and defend the trees. He didn't understand how trees were in danger since there were trees everywhere he went; but he trusted his elementary school teachers and determined that if trees needed saving, he wanted to be numbered among the tree savers.

During his time in Washington D.C. he had always fought for trees. If there were ever legislation having anything to do with saving trees, he was right in the middle of it. One time, Andrew rallied to fight a particularly bad piece of legislation that threatened trees; he and his allies had produced study after study proving without a doubt that the legislation was harmful. They delivered stacks and stacks of studies to those who supported the legislation to show they were wrong. Their goal had been to overwhelm them with paperwork and studies and it eventually worked.

Despite his established record on the defense of trees, but Andrew was keenly aware that he had never directly saved one. He had helped the smaller trees by providing them sunlight, but he hadn't necessarily saved them. In his work in the legislature, he had only fought for procedures or committees that would increase the likelihood of saving trees. Now, he had a chance to physically save a tree that was right in front of him.

He put on his boots and coat and walked to the base of the tree. All of the branches had at least two feet of snow on them. He could see several branches bending down so much that they were pointing at the ground. The lowest branch nearly touched the ground.

"Don't worry. I'm going to save you," He said, stroking the bark on the tree trunk.

He picked a long stick off the ground and approached a burdened tree branch that seemed ready to give in to the weight. He stood underneath and raised the stick to poke at the snow. With a few quick pokes, the snow fell off the branch and onto his head.

To Andrew's surprise, as soon as he relieved the branch of the oppressive snow it whipped up violently and let out a loud snapping noise that echoed throughout the snow-covered valley. The large branch fell with a thud to the ground and rested at Andrew's feet.

Staring in amazement and shock, he couldn't believe that such a large branch would snap like that. "What was that about?"

He walked over to the branch and knelt down to examine the break. The outside of the branch was completely coated with ice.

"The ice! That's the problem. I need to get that ice off or the trees will freeze."

He spent the next few days knocking ice off the trunks and branches of the trees close to camp. He thought the most important thing was to get the ice off of the trunks so he paid special attention to making sure he removed the ice and kept it off.

This project gave him something to do throughout the rest of the winter. Every couple of days he would check the trees for ice and whenever he found some, he would chip it off as best he could.

Andrew kept scrupulous notes about his activities with the trees, as he did with all his other activities. He documented everything he did and included his own commentary and conclusions. Andrew concluded that the tree de-icing project had surely saved the tall tree and prolonged the life expectancies of the smaller trees.

## Chapter 19: The Reckoning

Weeks had gone by since Andrew checked on the squirrels. He hadn't seen them for a while so he decided to make sure the thin squirrel still had enough nuts to survive. He strode over to the thin squirrel's tree while scanning the area for any signs of life. He didn't see him and didn't see any nutshells at the bottom of the tree. Andrew was suddenly concerned. He pulled himself up on the lowest branch and put his head right up to the thin squirrel's nest.

Quickly, he pulled his head away from the hole and looked away. Hunching on the tree branch, he put his head between his knees. The air was crisp and the wind was almost completely still. He kept his head down and started breathing heavily. Then, without warning, he vomited.

The thin squirrel lay dead inside his nest in the tree. The body was partially decomposed and the stench inside the tree trunk was potent. The decomposing body was curled up in a ball on top of a sizable stash of nuts.

"How did this happen? I gave him everything he needed. How could he die when he had plenty of nuts in his nest?"

Confusion turned to sadness as he realized he had lost an ally in the squirrel community. Andrew wanted the squirrels to trust and befriend him and the thin squirrel had been his chance. He liked believing the thin squirrel would look to him as a provider and protector. What he did for the squirrel wasn't difficult - all he did was take some nuts from the fat squirrel and drop them in the thin squirrel's nest - but just the fact that he did it should have earned him some praise and trust. Now he had nothing to show for it.

"I should have kept those nuts for myself," he thought. "It's not like the fat squirrel needed them! He was just fine with all of his stashes. That greedy, overreaching wretch who was stealing from all the good squirrels must have caused this in some way."

Disappointed, Andrew went back to camp and sat by the fire to think about the situation.

"That was a waste of time. How will I earn trust with the squirrels now?"

Questions still loomed in Andrew's mind. He couldn't figure out what had happened or why.

"Maybe the thin squirrel was so intimidated by

the evil fat squirrel that he didn't want to eat his nuts even though I had given them to him. Maybe the thin squirrel wouldn't eat the nuts because I touched them, which is the fat squirrel's fault for causing me to have to take them to the thin squirrel's nest."

Andrew glared at the tree that housed the fat squirrel's nest. He pictured the fat squirrel sitting back in that nest with hundreds of nuts, not having to worry about the cold because of its fat, blubbery insulation. Annoyance at the fat squirrel's greed was turning into vile hatred.

"That greedy fatty!" He thought, clinching his teeth. "He was all snug in his nest with plenty of food and warmth while the thin squirrel was freezing and starving to death."

Walking toward the fat squirrel's tree, he wasn't sure what he would do, but he knew he had to at least disturb him and tell him what he'd done. When he reached the tree, he pulled himself up on a limb and climbed two more branches until he was high enough to look inside the nest.

He looked in the nest and saw a thin squirrel curled up in a ball. There were no nuts in the nest and the squirrel appeared to be sleeping. Andrew was shocked by how thin the fat squirrel had become.

"How will this guy survive after losing so much weight?"

Looking closer, however, he saw that the squirrel

had *not* survived. Much like the thin squirrel, the previously fat squirrel was dead and its body had started to decompose. The squirrel's fur still covered the body, but it was mangy and thin.

Andrew climbed down from the tree more confused now than angry. He sauntered back to camp and sat down again by the fire. He could feel that temperatures were dropping and a storm would most likely be coming through.

"What could have caused both squirrels to die? It's clear that the fat squirrel killed the thin squirrel with his greed, but how did the fat squirrel die?"

After pondering the question for nearly an hour, he wasn't able to come up with any reasonable explanations short of some sort of squirrel epidemic. Snow had begun falling and the wind had picked up, so he put out the fire and returned to his tent.

"At least fairness has been achieved. That's all that really matters," Andrew thought sadly as he zipped the door shut.

As he lay in his tent still thinking about the day's events, a sound ripped through the valley that was unmistakable, followed by a tremor that felt like an earthquake. Andrew jumped to his window to peer out at the whiteout. The tall tree had been taken down by the wind with ease. It had narrowly missed Andrew's tent and landed on his fire pit. The tree had landed on and destroyed one of his chairs and made a mess of his campsite. He shuddered as he thought of how close it came to the tent.

The next morning when the storm passed, he inspected the break in the tree trunk. He couldn't tell what had happened; it looked like it had been snapped in half at the base.

"I guess it was just a really old tree."

Andrew felt sad for the tree. He knelt down next to it and gazed at it sympathetically.

"I did everything I could to save you. I thinned your branches on one side last spring and removed the snow from your branches and the ice from your trunk. What more could I have done?"

He stood up and started walking back to the tent.

"Nothing. There is nothing more I could have done. At least it fell near the fire pit. Now I can use it for firewood and I don't have to carry it far."

Andrew knew he would miss the tall tree, but decided to focus on the positive by pointing out that now the smaller trees would get all the sunlight they wanted.

# Chapter 20: The Trap

By the end of winter, Andrew had cleared the tall tree and cut the majority of it into more firewood than he could possibly need. Though the winter had proven to be more constructive than the previous winter had been, Andrew welcomed the return of spring gladly. Once again, the animals reappeared and new life was abundant in the valley. Though there were notably fewer deer roaming the valley, there was a new fawn prancing around with its mother. Baby chicks chirped in nests overhead and flowers budded throughout the valley.

To Andrew's delight, he had also seen Gray Protector a few times as he started his usual exploring routes. He had only seen him twice in the year and a half he had been in the valley but was thrilled to have caught a glimpse of him four times in the past two weeks. Andrew felt that Gray Protector trusted him now and could see that Andrew loved him and wanted to be friends.

Though the wolf still kept his distance, Andrew began tracking when and where he saw Gray Protector to figure out his habits.

One day, while looking for Gray Protector, he came across some wild blackberries. Andrew didn't get much fruit in his diet so he stopped to fill up and take some back to camp. As he was picking berries, he noticed an animal approaching him from the other side of the blackberry bushes. He thought it must be Gray Protector coming to greet him. He looked up and was shocked to see Evan lumbering towards the blackberry bush.

Evan halted upon seeing Andrew. They stood only twenty yards from each other. Andrew, still feeling empowered from the encounter in the cave, stood his ground and yelled at Evan.

"Haven't you figured it out yet? Get away from me! Stay away from here!"

Andrew hadn't brought his rifle with him, because he only anticipated seeing Gray Protector. He had no way of protecting himself against Evan so he grabbed a handful of blackberries and threw them at him. Evan growled, stood on his hind legs and stretched out his arms. He towered over Andrew.

Fear struck through him. Despite his fear, Andrew noticed that Evan's claws hadn't grown back yet.

Evan growled again and Andrew panicked. He knew that running away from a bear was foolish, but he was so frightened he wasn't thinking straight.

Andrew turned his back and ran as fast as he could. He didn't have the courage to look behind to see if Evan was following; he just kept running while fully expecting to be taken down from behind at any moment.

After thirty seconds of running with no takedown, he stopped to look behind him. There was no sign of Evan. Andrew's heart was still pounding rapidly. He couldn't believe how big Evan was when he stood up. The whole incident caught him off guard and, now that he had time to reflect, he was upset by his own reaction.

"I shouldn't have backed down. It's about time someone took out that bully."

On the way back to camp he stewed about the encounter with Evan. He felt small again. All of the confidence and power that he had felt after the incident in the cave was now diminished and he needed to get it back.

He started carrying his rifle again when he went on his hikes. He desperately wanted to confront Evan again. On the second day of searching, however, Andrew came across a dead fawn whose body was ripped to shreds. The skin was still largely in tact, but most of the good meat had been ripped away by deep claw marks all over the poor fawn's body. It was a terrible sight.

"That's it," Andrew said with tears in his eyes. "I'm going to kill him!"

After much deliberation, he decided to make a bear trap using some extra rope. He had learned to make traps from his Boy Scout days and had practiced them on his brother when they were younger.

It was a simple trap and the key was to set it up in the right place with the right bait. Evan would probably be hanging around the blackberry bushes on a regular basis so he returned to the spot where Evan had snuck up on him and set the trap there.

He placed blackberries, trout and the fawn's carcass near the trap, carefully placing each item in optimal position to tempt the insatiable bear. The trap was about half a mile from Andrew's camp so he decided to make the hike a few times a day to check on it.

It had only been set up for four hours when Andrew heard a loud, frightening shrieking sound echo throughout the valley. He instantly knew he had caught something in the trap. Grabbing his rifle, he rushed to the trap.

As he got closer, he could hear something struggling nearby. It sounded like something big.

Andrew had already decided he wouldn't get

close to him until he had put a few bullets in his heart.

Using trees to block his approach, he got close enough to take aim at the trapped bear. Slowly, he peeked out from behind a tree and pointed his rifle toward the trap. To his horror, he saw Gray Protector struggling to get free from the rope that was wrapped around both of his hind legs.

Andrew didn't know what to say or do. He was ashamed he hadn't been more careful to make a trap specifically for Evan, so Gray Protector wouldn't have to get involved. Andrew hated himself for harming such a beautiful, innocent creature.

Under normal circumstances he was certain he could have just walked up to Gray Protector and stroked his fur, but because Gray Protector was so frightened, he thought it might upset him to get too close. Andrew knew he needed to get the rope untied without frightening his friend or hurting him any more than he already had.

He approached slowly and quietly. When the wolf saw Andrew approaching, he let out a loud yelp and started frantically trying to escape. Andrew put his hands out in front of him and tried to comfort the wolf.

"It's okay, buddy. You can trust me," he said. "Don't worry, I won't hurt you. I'm sorry I got you into this. I'm so sorry. This is my fault. You didn't do anything wrong."

## LIBERAL IN NATURE

The wolf continued his frantic behavior and as Andrew got closer it directed its ferocity at him. Gray Protector growled fiercely at Andrew and revealed his sharp fangs. He looked ready to pounce but was still confused and flustered. Andrew was frightened.

"This is my fault. I was careless in setting this up and now my chickens have come home to roost. My friend is suffering because of me. How can I make this right?"

Andrew knew he wouldn't be able to get close enough to loosen the tight loop around the wolf's legs, but he thought that if he cut the rope from where it was anchored, his frantic movements would loosen it.

He walked slowly and continued to try to comfort his friend.

"I'm just going to cut the rope," he said. "I'm going to cut the anchor and then you can loosen it. You'll be free. You can go back to what you were doing. Everything will be okay."

He reached the anchor and Gray Protector had calmed down slightly. Andrew cut the rope and backed away slowly. As soon as Grey Protector realized the rope was loose, he turned and ran. As he ran away the loop around his legs loosened and he broke off into a full sprint. He never looked back.

Andrew stood still and watched as Gray Protector disappeared and then he collapsed to the ground. He was experiencing shock, thrill, fear, excitement and relief all at the same time and it was too much for him to handle. He lay still on the ground for forty minutes before he heard a stick break about a hundred yards away.

Andrew thought he must be coming back to say thank you for freeing him. He rolled over on his side to greet Gray Protector, but instead saw Evan approaching. Andrew had been lying so still on the ground that Evan hadn't noticed him.

When Evan was fifty yards away, he stopped and sniffed the air. He seemed to smell Andrew's presence but hadn't pinpointed where he was. Sniffing again, he turned his back to Andrew.

A shot echoed in the valley as a bullet left Andrew's rifle and entered Evan's left lung. Evan jumped and scrambled to run when another shot rang out and a bullet shredded Evan's left shoulder. Two more quick shots echoed. Evan was on the ground panting furiously. He tried to stand, but couldn't. Bright red blood covered his black fur.

Andrew stood up, reloaded his rifle and shot four more bullets haphazardly into Evan's body. The bear lay motionless in a pool of blood.

Andrew looked at the limp body lying fifty yards away. After making sure he had all his items, he walked back to camp. Gray Protector was free and Evan was dead. Though Andrew did not revel in killing anything, he knew it was necessary.

"Sacrifices must be made. The valley is a better place now."

# Chapter 21: The Climate

One of Andrew's goals when arriving in the valley was to track the warming trends. From the day he arrived he had recorded the temperature in the valley three times a day. His goal was to track temperatures for an entire year and then compare temperatures with the previous year. If the second year temperatures were higher, as Andrew predicted they would be, it would further prove the already proven fact that man was causing the earth's temperature to rise.

Global warming had become a hobby of Andrew's in recent years. He had met many of the world's leading global warming scientists and had helped to discredit the so-called scientists who did not support global warming. Global warming was, in fact, one of his favorite things to debate with conservatives. It was such an easy argument to make

## LIBERAL IN NATURE

that conservatives were left with no leg to stand on.

He would typically start the debate by declaring that all reputable and distinguished scientists had proven that global warming is a fact. His conservative counterparts would then say something about other scientists to which Andrew would brilliantly reply, "Well, if a scientist doesn't believe in global warming, then he has no credibility and is therefore not reputable *or* distinguished. So who cares what he says?"

Andrew would then sit back and smile smugly as the conservatives tried to tell him something about circular arguments or fudged data. Of course, Andrew expected this kind of nonsense and he almost felt bad about having to play the ultimate trump card on his conservative opponent.

"Well, there are those who still deny the Holocaust. And here you are; denying global warming."

Andrew would then watch, as they would become frantic. Once on the defensive, conservatives could no longer stand with him. He would listen as they talked about $CO_2$ being necessary for life, how $CO_2$ levels actually trailed warming temperatures and how there was a global cooling alarm in the 1970s and all the other talking points they had picked up from Sean Hannity, Mark Levin, Monica Crowley, Jerry Doyle and all the other stooges. Andrew assumed all of that was false so after listening to their gibberish for a few minutes, he would finally drive the final nail in the coffin by saying "the science is settled!"

At that point anyone who still thought they had an argument was obviously someone who didn't deserve his time or attention. Unfortunately, typically the person would continue the argument and Andrew would be forced to throw them – or rather they would throw themselves – into the group labeled "idiots and imbeciles."

Andrew was excited to get involved in the fact gathering to further prove global warming. He had a friend who worked on Al Gore's staff; they had met and bonded at a fund raising celebration shortly after Mr. Gore won the Nobel Prize in 2007. He planned on sending his findings to his friend in the hopes that Mr. Gore might benefit from them.

Andrew had placed a thermometer on one of the tall tree's branches so he would have easy access recording the temperature each day. Every day he recorded the temperature around 8 AM, noon, and 5 PM. The spring after the freak storm took down the tall tree, Andrew was forced to move the thermometer up the mountain to his meditation spot.

In the beginning, recording the temperatures was just something to do; something to keep him busy, but the more he did it the more he enjoyed it. It helped him feel like a real scientist. He liked the routine and the structure of recording data and, after a while, he became obsessed with it. If he were out on a hike and time got away from him he would race back to camp so he could be there on time to record the temperature for the day. His recording of the weather was usually something simple such as, "scattered clouds, light rain, slight breeze from the south." On some days Andrew would elaborate on the weather conditions when he found them to be interesting or noteworthy.

After recording the temperature for a few months, Andrew was searching through his backpack and found the weather statistics he had printed off in preparation for his journey. The Wikipedia printouts gave detailed temperature statistics for the entire year. He started reviewing his calculations of the past months to come up with monthly averages and quarterly averages so he could compare them to the printout. To his delight, his temperatures seemed to be, on average, two degrees hotter than the averages on the printout.

Andrew was extremely meticulous in his record keeping. He compared his records with the Wikipedia printout and concocted detailed reports complete with explanations and conclusions. He did not know yet what he would do with his reports but he knew they would be of great benefit at some point. He copied all of his data into a formal presentation for his friend.

He thought that before the next autumn set in, he would hike to the nearest town and mail the data to his friend. Hopefully his research would help Mr. Gore immensely and he swelled with pride to think that he would read it someday soon.

A few weeks later, on a warm summer day, Andrew was making his usual rounds when a buzzing sound off in the distance startled him. He paused and listened carefully. The sound grew louder until it was clear to Andrew that a helicopter was approaching. He expected to see Arlen's old off-white piece of junk miraculously flying through the air, but was surprised when a shiny, blue helicopter started descending toward camp.

"Who is this and what is he doing here?"

Hurrying back to camp, he was surprised to find Arlen sitting in one of his chairs. Arlen stood when he saw Andrew approaching.

"Hey there, buddy. Just thought I'd check up on you and make sure you're alive and doing alright."

Andrew was caught off guard. This was the first human contact he'd had in a year and a half. He couldn't believe that someone was standing right in front of him, talking to him. Andrew hardly knew what to say.

"Thanks. New helicopter, huh?"

"Yeah, she's a beaut ain't she?" Arlen replied with a smile. "Business picked up so I picked up a respectable ride. She practically flies herself. How have you been?"

"I'm doing alright," Andrew said. "I'm getting things straightened up around here."

Andrew suddenly felt defensive. He didn't want to talk to any outsiders. He knew Arlen wouldn't understand his mission and would criticize him and his work in the valley. He just wanted him to leave so the valley could be restored to its natural condition.

"Why are you here? What do you want?"

"Don't want anything. Just checking in. You told me to check – "

"Never mind what I told you. I think it's best if you go back. I'm fine. Everything's fine. Just let me get back to my work."

Arlen looked at Andrew with concern. He didn't seem to know what to say or do.

"I brought some food. You interested? Homemade beef jerky and homemade trail mix. It's good stuff."

"Sure. That would be nice. Thank you."

Arlen's surprise visit had put Andrew in a melancholy mood. He was not expecting an outside visitor. He was happy to see him and also annoyed. He had almost forgotten that the outside world even existed. He had shut out most of his thoughts and questions of what was going on in society. Now that

Arlen was here, Andrew realized he didn't want any part of society to come to the valley.

Arlen walked to his helicopter and grabbed four large grocery bags full of jerky and trail mix.

"This should last you a while. Glad to know things are good. Thought about you all alone up here many times but didn't want to disturb you. I knew I was headed close to you today so I decided to pop in. Sorry to come unannounced but there's really no way to announce it anyway."

Arlen handed the bags to Andrew and then headed back to his helicopter. As he reached for the door, he asked, "Do you want me to take anything back for you? Any messages for your family?"

This again caught him off guard and he shook his head. Arlen waved and fired up the helicopter. The blades started turning and dust and debris began swirling around Andrew.

The helicopter had barely lifted off the ground when Andrew broke out of his daze.

"The studies!" he yelled.

He ran closer to Arlen's helicopter but was pelted with flying debris. He waved his arms frantically to try to get Arlen to put the helicopter down again. After a few seconds, Arlen saw him and brought the helicopter back down. Andrew ran to Arlen's door.

"Can you mail something for me?" he yelled to Arlen as he tried to catch his breath.

"Sure can!" Arlen yelled back.

Andrew ran to his tent and returned a few minutes later with a stack of papers, which he handed to Arlen.

"Will you put all of this in an envelope and mail it to this address?" Andrew said pointing to his friend's name and address.

"No problem, Chief. Anything else?"

"No. Just this. It's really important."

"I'll get 'er done, buddy."

"Thanks!"

With that, Arlen closed the door and the blades spun faster and faster as Andrew backed away. The helicopter lifted off the ground, banked and then headed west. Within a few minutes, Arlen was out of sight and the valley was back to normal.

Though he was annoyed by Arlen's intrusion, Andrew forgave him because of the service he provided. Andrew felt the universe had brought Arlen to him at the right time because the climate data was so important for saving the environment. He felt relief knowing all of the research was out of his hands and on its way to the hands of those who could apply it.

Having completed his climate change project, Andrew decided to return the thermometer to his camp. Though he would continue to record temperatures and weather he had already proven what he wanted to prove so he didn't care about being meticulous anymore.

He hiked up the hill to where the thermometer hung from a tree. As he unhooked the thermometer he noticed it read sixty-two degrees. He walked back to his camp and hung it on one of the smaller trees in camp. When he let go of it he noticed that the thermometer read fifty-seven degrees.

"Did a cold front just move in? How is it that the temperature just dropped five degrees during that thirty minute walk?"

He couldn't understand what had happened. As he stood there and thought about it, the temperature dropped another two degrees. Andrew was baffled. He wondered if the thermometer was broken or if maybe the elevation change could cause the drop in temperature.

"That's impossible though, because the temperature is supposed to be colder the higher you go. But in this case, the temperature is actually higher at the higher elevation."

He wondered if he'd just made a mistake when he first looked at the thermometer.

"Maybe the temperature was actually fifty-two degrees and then rose three degrees as I walked down the hill."

His curiosity got the better of him and the honorary scientist within him demanded that he try to re-create the phenomenon. He checked the thermometer again; it read fifty-five degrees. He unhooked it and hauled it back up the mountain to where it hung before. As he hung it up he noticed that the thermometer read fifty-nine degrees. He waited a few minutes and the temperature went up to sixty-two degrees – just as it had when he first took it from the spot about an hour before.

Andrew couldn't believe what he was seeing. The temperature stayed steady at sixty-two as the thermometer hung from a tree on the hill about a third of the way from the valley floor. He again unhooked the thermometer from the tree and carried it back down to camp. This time as he walked he watched the thermometer. Just about every couple hundred yards the temperature dropped half a degree until he got back to camp and hung it on the same tree. It settled at fifty-five degrees.

There appeared to be an average difference of seven degrees between the tree location at his camp and the tree location on the hill. Andrew hurriedly found his temperature book and looked at his comparisons and analysis. He noticed that the difference in temperature from year one to year two on average was about seven and a half degree increase. He fretted.

"If there is a seven-degree difference between the two locations and my calculations show an average increase of seven degrees, that would suggest that this year's temperature was actually half a degree cooler than the previous year. That's impossible."

Andrew poured over his notes furiously to try to reconcile the problem. He double checked everything and still couldn't make sense of it. He didn't know what to think.

"How could there be a *decrease* in temperature? That's just not possible. Science says that as you go up in elevation, the temperature will decrease, but the amount of elevation between the tree on the hill and this tree isn't significant enough to make a big difference. It doesn't make sense scientifically so there must be some sort of problem with the thermometer."

He sat down on his folding chair and thought about the dilemma. He tried to come up with explanations that would account for this situation and still support his conclusions. He couldn't explain any of it.

"Perhaps I made a mistake in recording my temperatures," he concluded. It was difficult for him to admit that *perhaps* he had made a mistake, but it was either that or admit that the numbers were right and the temperature was not rising. That would make him a borderline climate change denier.

"One year is a very small sample size. It's not enough to determine anything. There are a number of factors that could account for discrepancies. It isn't an incredibly reliable study at this point."

He then thought of the report that he sent to his friend on Al Gore's staff.

"What will he say? What would he do if he knew about this discrepancy? With all those conclusions and all the comparisons, somebody might discover the discrepancy and then those crazy conservatives will have some ammunition against the science."

He worried about embarrassing Mr. Gore or his team who had worked so hard and been so honest and accurate about everything dealing with global warming. He thought of writing another letter telling his friend to disregard his report but he eventually concluded that it would just cause confusion and conflict and would require him to travel several days to deliver the message. So, he decided to let it go and reassured himself that it would all get worked out in the end.

"Besides, since global warming has already been proven as fact and since my report only worked to support that fact; it's okay that part of it was based on questionable data. Neptune's bones are still dissolving," he said, quoting his favorite poem.

The conclusion he decided was correct; and the method of arriving at that conclusion was not as important. In addition, he hadn't mentioned in the report that he had moved the thermometer up the hill, so no one would be able to figure out what really happened anyway!

With that disaster averted, his enthusiasm returned and his excitement at the prospect of being included in some of Mr. Gore's work grew more than it had before. After chalking the entire episode up to being a big misunderstanding, he never recorded the temperature again.

# Chapter 22: The Attack

The end of summer was approaching. Something had changed in the valley that Andrew couldn't quite comprehend. He had discovered a few deer carcasses throughout the valley – killed in the same manner as the others he had found previously with their remains scattered all around. Evan had been dead for a few weeks, but he figured he must have killed them before he died.

Still, the deer must not have known of Evan's death, because they had seemingly left the valley altogether. Andrew hadn't seen a single deer since Evan died. He felt alone and thoughts of returning to society started creeping into his mind once again.

Ever since Arlen had broken the utopian spell he had been under, his curiosity had been growing about what was going on in the world. He didn't know why, but he was extremely anxious about something.

Strange things happening in the valley strengthened Andrew's anxiety. One day he returned from a long hike to discover that the three smaller trees for which he had provided sunlight had all dried up and fallen to the ground. Squirrels should have been scurrying around his camp getting ready for fall but there were no squirrels in sight. The deer were gone and even the trout fishing had slowed down significantly. Midges and stoneflies hatched in such abundance morning and evening that Andrew had to stay inside his tent to avoid being swarmed.

The only animal Andrew saw on a somewhat regular basis was the wolf. Andrew was glad he had regained Gray Protector's trust, which helped him forget some of the other strange phenomena in the valley. He was a loyal friend who wouldn't abandon him.

Andrew was disappointed with the deer though. He had a suspicion they left because they feared Gray Protector. Andrew wished he could tell the deer that Evan, the predator, was dead and there was no need to fear Gray Protector.

The deer, however, had made their choices and Andrew thought it made them look petty and bigoted. They judged the wolf because of his sharp teeth, long claws and sleek fur. They didn't know anything about him and allowed their irrational prejudice to take control.

"Good riddance," Andrew muttered to himself. "I can't believe I mistook them for wise creatures."

Andrew was struggling for purpose now that most of the animals were gone and the trees were falling down. He went for a walk one evening to clear his mind and look for signs of life. Walking along the river, he hoped to see fish rising to the surface or deer drinking the water. All he saw was swarms of stoneflies. The valley was starting to look depressing to him. All of the vibrancy it once had was gone. The animals, trees and plants had once looked so fresh and lively and now everything was drab and lifeless.

Andrew traced the downturn of the valley to either Evan or possibly the squirrel sickness. It was Evan who had thrown off the balance though. He had killed the deer, eaten the fish and frightened the other animals. His constant clawing of the trees most likely made them fall. Even though Andrew had heroically disposed of Evan, the affects of his greed and arrogance would take time to work themselves out of the valley.

As he continued his walk along the river, he saw something moving stealthily ahead of him. He stopped to get sight of the creature. At this point, he was excited to see any sign of life. He hoped the movement could be the beginning of something new.

Stepping out from behind some brush his eyes locked with Gray Protector's.

"Oh, it's you," Andrew said. "You startled me."

He stared into the eyes of the creature but the creature looked away. It was looking off into the distance as if pondering some important question. This comforted Andrew and put him at ease.

Andrew smiled at the wolf but the wolf still looked pensively off into the distance as if in a trance. Andrew did not want to disturb his friend so he turned his back and took a few steps towards camp. As he turned away from the wolf, its eyes darted from the distance and focused directly on Andrew's back. Andrew had only taken three steps when the wolf had sunk its claws into his back and leveled Andrew's body with its snout.

Andrew had no time to think about what was happening. He was stunned by the takedown and was as still as one can be while suffering a wolf attack. Andrew realized that there were more wolves approaching him from the sides. He started scrambling to get free, but stopped because he didn't want to hurt any wolves. He curled into a ball with his face in the dirt and his hands protecting his head. The wolves were panting loudly and he could feel their breath on his neck. They were ready to move in for the kill.

Andrew, realizing that he was in danger, cried out to Gray Protector.

"Why? Why are you doing this? I am your

friend!" He shouted.

One of the wolves bit hard into his ankle and tried to drag Andrew on the ground. Its jaws were clenched so tight Andrew thought the bones of his feet would be crushed. He tried to collect his thoughts. Everything seemed like it was happening in slow motion.

"What triggered this attack? No, this is not an attack. This is a mistake. He did not *mean* to attack me. He isn't violent and isn't a threat. This is all a misund..."

His thoughts were interrupted by a loud bang followed by a terrifying yelp. The pressure and gnawing ceased at once and he heard padded footsteps running away from him. A few more bangs rang out followed by more yelps. The yelp he heard next to him was now a faint whimper. Though he was in tremendous pain he managed to look toward the sound. Gray Protector was standing on his front legs with his bloody hind legs lying limp on the ground. The wolf was attempting to stand but he couldn't move his hind legs. He managed to crawl a few feet but then fell down, continuing his whimpering.

Andrew was in shock. He couldn't tell what condition he was in. He knew his whole body was in pain and he felt warm liquid on his back. The pain, fear and surprise all combined to leave Andrew in a frozen state. He replayed the whole incident in his mind while replaying his whole life in one instant. Images and experiences flooded his mind so rapidly that he couldn't keep them straight.

Suddenly, he jumped back as a single gunshot sounded right next to him. He couldn't tell if he'd been shot but in all his panic he noticed that the whimpering had stopped. A gray-haired man was standing over Gray Protector with a smoking revolver. His mind couldn't process the scene before him.

"Who is that and where did he come from?"

The man put his revolver in a case by his side and turned to Andrew. Andrew knew there was nowhere to go and, given his condition, there was nothing he could do to defend himself. He just lay on the ground looking up at the man who was now taking steps toward him. When about three feet from Andrew, he stopped and knelt down.

Andrew looked at him carefully. The man had long gray hair and a full gray beard. His upper body was exposed to reveal sharp, defined muscles. He wore gray shorts that were covered in stains of all colors. His calves were also muscular and he wore no shoes. His face looked young – way too young to match the gray hair. His body seemed like the body of a thirty year-old. The man's face only had a few wrinkles. His forehead was large, as his hair appeared to have receded slightly. His eyes were grayish blue and penetrating. His nose was rounded and his lips were full.

The man's face was kind and wise. He seemed familiar; like a distant friend or family member who he hadn't seen for a long time and didn't know why. He wanted to embrace the man and thank him for his help, to cry and scream for joy at the same time. Andrew's heart began to burn within him and his body tingled. He couldn't understand what was happening.

Reaching out his hand to Andrew he asked, "Are you okay?"

Andrew, struggling to lift his arm, shook his hand and was alarmed by the sensation of being shocked by electricity. "Who is this guy?" Andrew thought to himself.

"My name is Michael," the man said.

Andrew clung to Michael's hand. It was like he was holding hands with a marble statue. He had a vice-like grip but didn't hurt Andrew's hand. He put the perfect amount of pressure on his hand to make him secure but not uncomfortable.

"I'm Andrew. I'm a liberal," Andrew said, as he drifted out of consciousness.

# Chapter 23: The Hermit

Michael carried Andrew to his camp and placed him gently on his air mattress. Gaining consciousness, Andrew was becoming more aware of the pain in his body.

"Do you have a first aid kit?" Michael asked.

"Yes. In the bin in the corner."

The man retrieved the kit and started cleaning and bandaging Andrew's wounds. Andrew still wasn't sure how bad it was, but he knew he had significant damage to his back and left foot.

Michael seemed skilled at first aid and Andrew was starting to feel better already. His mind was full of questions for the man, but he didn't dare ask them.

"You have some serious damage to your ankle," Michael said. "You'll need to stay off of it for a few weeks."

"But, how will I continue all of my projects?" Andrew asked in a concerned voice. "What am I going to do? I can't just sit here all by myself for weeks."

"Don't worry. I will stay with you, if you need me."

Andrew wasn't sure how he felt about camping with a complete stranger in the middle of nowhere, but then this man didn't seem like a stranger. Normally he would have balked at the idea, but Andrew felt like he could trust him.

Andrew was still marveling at Michael's sudden appearance. He had no idea what to think of the situation. Countless questions continued to swirl in his mind. Finally, he couldn't hold back any longer.

"Who are you?" Andrew asked, trying to tone down his amazement.

"I'm just an old hermit," the man said with a smile.

"How did you find me?" Andrew inquired.

"I've seen your camp a few times over the past year or so. I just haven't wanted to bother you. You seemed like you were doing fine on your own."

"How did you know I needed help today?" Andrew asked.

"I didn't. I just felt like I should go for a walk along the eastern ridge. When I arrived at the edge of the ridge I saw the wolves moving in on you and I came to help."

"What are you doing up here?" Andrew asked.

"There will be time for answers. You need to rest now. I will be taking care of you for a while so I can answer all your questions in time. You will probably be sick of hearing me talk by the time you're healed."

Michael left Andrew alone. The shock and adrenaline had worn off and Andrew was starting to feel the pain of his injuries, but he desperately wanted to find out more about Michael and what he was doing in the wilderness. He felt a connection with him unlike any other he had experienced in his life. Andrew felt that they must be connected by a common purpose and ideology.

"Maybe he came here for the same reason I did," Andrew thought. "He lives in the wilderness, he helps those who are in need of help, and he seems wise. He must be a liberal like me."

Andrew's hopes increased as he thought about how much good he and Michael could do in the valley as a team. He thought Michael could bring wisdom and experience to Andrew's cause. He wanted to tell Michael about all of his work in the valley. His mind wandered as he drifted off to sleep.

Andrew awoke to the aroma of something cooking. Something sizzled outside and the aroma made his stomach grumble. He tried to sit up but the pain in his back was too much to handle.

Michael entered the tent with a plate of steaming food. Andrew devoured the food and felt much better. All of the same questions came back to his mind and he couldn't resist asking them.

"Why are you here in the wilderness?"

"Because I was foolish and immature many years ago."

"What happened? What brought you here?"

"I was a lawyer a long time ago. I had a young family and a solo law practice in a small town. I had three kids under six years old and a beautiful wife. I liked the law but did not really enjoy the practice of it. I didn't like dealing with opposing lawyers, many of whom were unreasonable and harsh. It was very stressful running a law firm, dealing with clients, dealing with lawyers, while trying to care for and provide for a young family. I felt like I had the weight of the world on my shoulders."

"I endured many sleepless nights during that time. I was always stressed about a case or a client. I would wonder where the money would come from to pay the bills and about how I was doing as a husband and father. It was tough and I hated all the stress but I did it because I loved my family. I did it because I felt like I was building something that would bless them and help us live a decent life.

"One snowy day I got a call from the sheriff

informing me that my family had been killed in a car accident. I was left with nothing – an empty house, an empty heart and an empty life. Practicing law didn't really make sense anymore. Why would I continue doing something I hated when the reason for doing it was now gone? But, I didn't know what else to do to earn a living. I closed up my firm, sold the house and I have been living here ever since. I suppose I came here looking for something and trying to forget something. I have lived in these mountains for over thirty years and still don't think I've found it."

Michael paused and looked at the mountains around him as if the thing he was looking for might be there. He looked back down at the ground.

"At first I was angry with the truck driver who hit the car. I was angry with myself because I was convinced I could have done something to prevent it. Then, I was angry with God for letting it happen. My first year here was very dark, lonely and painful. Eventually, I learned to be one with the natural world around me. I learned to coexist with the animals and plants."

"What do you do?" Andrew asked. "How do you keep yourself busy and sane up here?"

"I mine for gold and silver. These rivers are full of gold flakes. I collect them and then I hike to the nearest town where I trade them for supplies. I usually go to town three times a year. Aside from that, I take walks, ponder, mourn and watch the animals."

"Do you ever think about going back?"

"Not anymore. The world has left me behind. I'm an old man now; I wouldn't know what to do down there. I can survive much better here than I would there."

"Where is your camp?"

"Several miles east of here. It's very modest and tucked away so you wouldn't notice it if you walked right by it. I just pass the time however I can. It's lonely, as I'm sure you know. I try to befriend the animals and serve them however I can."

"I have been doing that too," said Andrew. "I have developed strategies for making the valley more fair and equitable. I've worked on it for about a year and a half."

"Fair and equitable?" Michael asked inquisitively. "What have you been doing?"

He told Michael about some of the work he had been doing in the valley. The pain from his injuries made it difficult for Andrew to focus, so he didn't go into great detail. He pointed to where Michael could get his journal and read about each of the projects. Michael didn't ask any questions or make any comments; he just listened and nodded his head.

Over the next few days, Michael read Andrew's journals while taking care of him. Andrew was eager to know Michael's reaction to his work, but Michael never said anything. As Michael read portions of the journals, he would wander around the valley to see where each event had taken place.

Andrew's patience was waning. He wanted to know what Michael thought. After a few days of waiting for questions or praise for doing so much to help nature, he couldn't stand it any longer.

"What do you think about all the work I've done?"

"Very interesting," Michael responded.

"I could use some help. We could work together."

"I don't know how much use I could be to you. I don't have the same drive or ambition as you. I just like to enjoy nature and let it work."

"That's how I used to be, but then I saw all of the problems that nature hadn't corrected so I decided to help. I feel it's my calling here."

"Very interesting," Michael responded. "What did you do before you came here? What brought you here?"

Even after almost two years, election night was still a difficult thing for Andrew to recall. He hadn't thought about it for some time, but couldn't avoid thinking about it now.

"I was in politics. I did fundraising, marketing and campaign management. In my earlier years, I worked in Washington D.C. as a legislative assistant. I devoted my career to helping those who couldn't help themselves. My political positions are based on doing what's best for people, especially those who don't know what's best for them."

"Things were going great until the most recent elections. I couldn't stand to witness a conservative president ruin the country so I fled. I had a dream about this valley and felt the calling to come here and use the skills I developed in my career to assist the plants and animals. I answered the call and here I am."

"At first, I just watched the animals and tried to coexist with them. But, I learned to recognize the inequalities and resolve them. I have fundamentally transformed this valley into a place of fairness and equality. The animals rely on me for support and help. I have done what God would do if he actually existed. I guess that sort of makes me the God of this valley."

Andrew looked at the old hermit. Michael looked troubled but Andrew couldn't tell what his concern was. Michael just stared down at the ground silently. Andrew suddenly became worried that the hermit didn't share his enthusiasm for helping the animals. He worried that Michael may not even be a liberal. He was upset that he had opened himself up – thinking that Michael was a political ally – only to have the old hermit attack him and his ideas.

Andrew immediately became defensive. He had to protect himself from the inevitable jabs that were coming. Instead of withdrawing, though, he went on the offensive. His instincts kicked in and it seemed to him that he hadn't been away from politics for a day.

"Is it really possible that I'm stuck in the wilderness with a freaking conservative?" Andrew wondered.

He had to know Michael's politics.

# Chapter 24: The Debate

Andrew spent the day resting inside his tent. Michael made food for him and helped him with his wounds. Michael had extensive knowledge about the various types of plants in the valley and the healing power each possessed. When he would redress Andrew's bandages, he would put some type of plant in the bandage. Andrew wasn't sure what they were, but they seemed to help.

Later in the evening, Michael built a fire and carried Andrew to one of his chairs. Michael had gathered firewood and stacked it by the fire.

"It's nice to get some fresh air," Andrew said.

"This air can heal a lot of ailments," Michael replied.

Still anxious to know where Michael stood on several issues, Andrew couldn't resist asking the questions that were constantly on his mind.

"When you were living in society, what were your political feelings? Which party did you align with?"

"I didn't really have a party. I thought they were both right and both wrong. I was never one for politics. It is such a deceptive game. I have opinions and principles that I rely on but mainly I believe in the power of the individual. I believe in the free exercise of God-given rights."

Michael's answer disappointed Andrew and revealed all Andrew needed to know about the man. He had heard this sort of nonsense many times so he didn't have to think about his response.

"What God-given rights are you talking about? Who is God that I should have to try to figure out what rights he allegedly gave me? Besides, the men who usually obtain these rights for themselves almost immediately use them to oppress and restrict the rights of others. Look at the Founders of this nation; they were so unhappy about the oppression of the Brits that they declared their independence and fought for their rights all the while holding the chains of their slaves. What about the slaves' rights? Where was God then?"

Andrew paused to assess the reaction of his opponent. He was usually able to shut people up with that line of defense and he wondered if the old hermit would make an attempt to go further. Andrew hoped he wouldn't press the issue. He didn't want to have to

## LIBERAL IN NATURE

embarrass the man who had saved him.

"What you say is partially true. There were complications in those days that I don't think we can fully appreciate, but it still makes it hard to accept. But, just because those men had slaves does not mean that the principles they fought for and established for this nation are any less true."

"It absolutely does. They were hypocrites. There's nothing worse than a hypocrite. Besides, the rights we have are given by the Constitution, which was established by the government. So, it is the government that grants those rights; not God or any other mystical nobody."

"Perhaps we should talk about something else. You're still recovering. I don't want you to get too excited or agitated."

"I'm fine. I just hate this talk about God-given rights and the power of the individual as if individuals can just choose their own selfish path and leave everyone else behind. Most people don't have the first clue what is good for them. That's where government comes in. People still have their freedom; the government just provides guidelines and safety nets."

"I agree that not all individuals know what is best for them, but who is anyone else to tell those people what is best for them? People make mistakes and hopefully learn from them. That's how progress really happens. That is how people learn what *is* best for them. If they don't have the freedom to make mistakes, how can they ever achieve their full potential?"

Andrew shifted in his chair. The pain in his back shot through his body as he moved, but he ignored it and continued the argument.

"So are we to just turn everyone loose? Every man for himself? Hooray for the power of the individual? What about the power of society? Wouldn't Jesus want to help people? How about 'What would Jesus do'? That's what I don't get about Christians; they claim to be so religious and then they turn their backs on the poor and needy. They're just a bunch of hypocrites."

The old hermit looked at Andrew inquisitively. "Do you know the Bible?"

"I know enough. I was forced to go to Sunday School when I was a kid."

"So what do *you* think Jesus would do?"

"He wouldn't be a greedy, racist homophobe."

"What *would* he be?"

"If He were real, He would help people. He would go out of his way to make sure there was no suffering, no war, and no pain. He would protect those who can't protect themselves. He would eliminate inequality and unfairness. He would heal everyone and make this world a better place."

"So, you *do* believe in Him?"

"I never said that. I'm just speaking from the beliefs of Christians since they are the ones who believe all these things and they are the ones who do the opposite."

"Isn't it a bit unfair to use their own God against them when you don't even believe in Him? That just seems a bit hypocritical as well. It would be one thing if you believed in Him and believed all those things you said about what He would do, but since you don't believe those things and since you don't believe in Him, can you really speak to what He would do if He were here?"

"I am just making the point that their "Savior" taught certain things and they don't even follow them."

"Perhaps if you look a little deeper, you will understand a bit more. Jesus didn't heal *everyone* and in fact instructed His disciples to not teach and heal certain groups of people. Jesus didn't say there would be no suffering. Jesus didn't promise people they would not experience pain. He didn't say life would be fair and equal. How would you even define equality? Jesus certainly didn't. He tried to make the world a better place but didn't force anyone.

He taught, exhorted and encouraged, but never forced anyone to be charitable. He gave people choices and explained consequences and let them govern themselves. He did not get involved in the government. He did not pass civil laws or play politics. He rendered unto Caesar what was Caesars. He railed against politicians and those who did good to be seen of their fellowmen. Even when He healed, it wasn't a free handout. His healings were earned through faith and usually followed with an encouragement to "sin no more" or to follow Him. When various people came to Him he sometimes responded with love and mercy and yet He sometimes responded with sternness and justice.

Why He chose one or the other, none of us knows, but we do know that He knew the hearts and minds of those people and we can assume He did and said what was needed in order to help the individual. Sometimes He presented a test for someone to pass or fail. Sometimes He simply offered an invitation. He knew the difference and He knew when to use one over the other, or something in between. The point is, no one knows what Jesus would do in a given situation because we don't have His perfect mind and we don't know the hearts and minds of the people around us. So, we probably shouldn't invoke Jesus into political discussions to support our point of view - especially if we don't actually believe in Him."

Michael finished and looked at Andrew, who was staring at the floor as if he hadn't heard anything the man said.

"Religion is responsible for so much of the world's suffering," Andrew said suddenly. "So many wars have been fought, so many people killed, so much hatred; all in the name of religion."

"Perhaps. But perhaps those wars were fought and those people killed because of man's need for power. Political motivations are almost always at the center of wars. Pure religion seeks to help men and women overcome that lust for power. It focuses on selflessness and humility. Men go to war when they ignore pure religion and succumb to their own carnal lusts for power and glory.

While it is true that some use religion as a banner to justify their own selfish desires, you can hardly blame the religion itself. Religion doesn't take away man's agency. It doesn't force people to agree with it. If you want to go, you can go. If you don't want to go, you don't go. If you want to donate money to the church, temple or synagogue, you can. If you don't want to donate money, you don't have to. Each person has his or her own choice and pure religion strives to influence people to make selfless choices that will lead to long-term happiness, rather than short-term pleasure."

Andrew was getting tired of the man's lectures. He hated that Michael was so calm but also firm. He usually would have been able to rile a guy up or make him give up by now. He could do neither to this hermit and it upset him.

Michael seemed to sense Andrew's annoyance. He smiled at Andrew and said; "tell me more about your work here."

"I have been observing the animals and trying to make this valley a better place."

Michael looked up and raised his eyebrows in surprise.

"A better place?" He said. "What was lacking?"

"I don't know if I'd say something was lacking, except that I thought some of the animals were disadvantaged. There were some...injustices here that I thought should not exist.

"What kinds of injustices?"

"I just thought that some of the animals were making it hard for the other animals to scrape out a living. Some of the animals had more than enough food and water while others barely had enough to live. It seemed like things were out of balance."

"Very interesting," said the old hermit. "I read about some of it in your journal. I was fascinated by all you have done here. In what ways do you feel you have made things better?"

Andrew tried to hide his annoyance at being questioned. He knew the best way to stop the questions was to lay out all he had done to improve the valley. He started with the day he saved the deer and continued by explaining even the intricate systems developed to help the disadvantaged animals. He explained his philosophies and the reasons behind his actions.

Michael sat and listened almost motionless. At times he looked up at Andrew to show he was still listening, but did not give any indication as to whether he approved of or disapproved of Andrew's work. He just listened and looked down at the fire.

When Andrew finished his explanation he looked up at the man.

"How do you know what is good for this valley? What makes you think things were out of balance? Don't you think Mother Nature knows how to balance herself? After all, this world is quite old and things have been working for millions of years without your help."

"Well, first of all, I don't believe that "Mother Nature" is a thing or person. I think the world is governed by science and science alone. So, I don't think that Mother Nature can consciously balance things out like a person balancing a checkbook. We control what happens and what doesn't happen. I don't believe in destiny and I don't believe in fate. I believe in looking at what's in front of me and making the right decision. I believe in being compassionate and helping those who are in need of help."

"And what is compassion?"

Andrew wondered if this man was really as simple as he sounded. "Does he not know the meaning of the word?" Can backcountry people really be this ignorant? He *must* be a Republican."

"Compassion is helping others," Andrew said almost embarrassed for the man. "It is a feeling of deep sympathy and sorrow for another who is stricken by misfortune, accompanied by a strong desire to alleviate the suffering."

"I know what the word means, but how do *you* apply it? How do *you* know when you are being compassionate?"

Andrew tried to hide his contempt for the man's ignorance, but it proved too difficult.

"Well. If you are alleviating suffering, then you are being compassionate. It's not very complicated."

"I disagree."

"You disagree? How can you disagree that alleviating suffering is compassionate? Anyone with half a brain must agree on that."

"I disagree that it's not very complicated."

"They're the same thing. If you understand the definition, then you can clearly deduce whether someone is being compassionate and it is, therefore, not complicated at all. A three year-old could get it."

Andrew was now perturbed and tired of the man's

ignorance. He felt like he *was* talking to a three year-old, except that three year-olds had an excuse for their ignorance. It was a worthless conversation, which is why Andrew typically conversed with people of intelligence and people with similar high ideals.

"What I mean is; how do you know when someone or something needs help? And how do you determine that your idea of help is help?"

"It is just obvious when something needs help. I don't really have to figure anything out. It just *is*."

"Okay, let me give you an example. You told me that you helped a thin squirrel. I assume that because the squirrel was sick, that would make it stricken with misfortune. Would you agree?"

"Yes."

"And you had deep sympathy and sorrow for it. Correct?"

"Yes"

"So you took some nuts from another squirrel to help the thin squirrel. Right?"

"Yes," Andrew knew where he was going with this and he already had an answer ready for him. He knew the man would ask him if it was compassionate toward the fat squirrel to take nuts from him. It was a classic argument that heartless conservatives usually made.

"Was that compassionate toward the other

squirrel?" The man asked.

"The fat squirrel had plenty and to spare. He was fat and he had about fifteen stashes of nuts. So, he wasn't really in need of compassion. In fact, he should have been compassionate and either left some nuts for others or given some of the nuts to the thin squirrel. I don't really think the compassionless are deserving of compassion."

"Okay. Was it compassionate toward the fat squirrel's four babies?"

This was an unexpected question and, though it was utterly ridiculous, Andrew was taken off guard. It was difficult to do this; he was trained to think immediately how to spin things. He tried to think of some response, but the question was so crazy he struggled to respond.

"What? What are you talking about? How could you possibly know that the squirrel had babies?"

"I looked in the squirrel's nest. What I saw was the skeleton of one large squirrel and four tiny squirrel skeletons inside the large skeleton. Therefore, I deduced that either the large squirrel was pregnant when *she* died, or she ate four baby squirrels just before her death. However, since it was not the time of the season for baby squirrels to be running around and since the baby squirrels were still too small to be born, I concluded that they were fetuses."

Andrew looked at the man in disbelief. He

couldn't believe what he was hearing.

"Baby squirrel skeletons? Andrew thought to himself. "This man is absolutely delusional."

"What kind of a person goes around prodding squirrel skeletons? That's completely insane."

"Maybe. But you haven't answered my question. How compassionate was it for you to take nuts from the "fat" squirrel to give them to the thin squirrel? If you had looked closely, you may have noticed that *he* was actually a *she* and that her weight was much lower in her body than an obese squirrel. If you had done this, you may have realized that the pregnant squirrel was collecting more nuts than the other squirrels because she had four fetuses in her womb and needed extra nourishment to feed them. So, your compassion toward the thin squirrel deprived the pregnant squirrel of the extra nourishment needed to support herself and her litter. You tried to save one squirrel, but instead killed five squirrels and the squirrel that you tried to save died anyway. So, I ask again, how do you determine who needs help and what constitutes help?"

Andrew just stared at the man. He felt flustered, but every moment it was turning to anger. The man took the opportunity to continue talking.

"I've seen this behavior before from animals, including squirrels. They just sit on the side and don't collect any nuts. I have wondered why they do that? I have pondered on that for many seasons of watching these squirrels. I have come to a conclusion, which I admit may or may not be correct. I think it comes down to compassion. That squirrel is *truly* compassionate. It knows that it will not last the winter. It knows its fate is to die."

Michael paused, looked down at the ground, and then started speaking again.

"So, rather than going about selfishly collecting nuts that it knows it will not need, it leaves them for others to collect. Sure the nuts could sustain the squirrel for a bit longer, but its ultimate fate is sealed so it sits and watches as other squirrels collect the nuts. In this case, the thin squirrel was leaving the nuts, not just for one squirrel, but for five squirrels. And, based on what you have said about the relationship between the thin squirrel and the pregnant squirrel, the thin squirrel may have even been doing this for his own offspring. That is compassion. And yet, his compassion was thwarted by your "compassion". His sacrifice and compassion was for naught."

Andrew was raging with contempt now. How could this strange man question his methods and effectiveness?

"That is an interesting theory, but I don't buy it for a second. I think you have spent too much time out here alone. Why are you here anyway? You couldn't make it out in the real world? You couldn't keep a job so you deserted and came out here to live out your fantasies and make-believe? You must be either crazy or senile, but I won't sit here and listen to anymore of your nonsense."

"I'm not criticizing you. I'm not trying to make you feel bad. I am only trying to open your eyes to different possibilities."

"*You* are trying to open *my* eyes? Are you kidding me? I am an educated man and I have worked for some of the most powerful people in the world. Who are you? You ran away and hid in isolation because something bad happened to you. Who do you think you are?"

"I am nobody. All I have done is try to live an honest life and be true to God."

Andrew laughed and looked at Michael as if he had just figured out something remarkable.

"Well, that explains everything, doesn't it? You are trying to be true to God. You devote your life trying to please a figment of your imagination. You cling to your religion and ignore facts, science and reason. How's that working out for you? Has God talked to you lately?"

"Yes."

"Really? God almighty has spoken to you, a lowly hermit? And what did he say to you?"

"I love you," Michael said solemnly.

"Pardon me? What are you talking about?"

"That's what God said to me. I love you."

"And how did He tell you that?"

"He didn't necessarily *tell* me that. He showed me. Every time I look at the beauty of the earth, I am reminded that God loves me because He created all of this for us to enjoy."

"Yeah, God created all of this. Evolution had nothing to do with it, right?"

"I didn't say that. It's quite possible that evolution had a lot to do with it, but I believe God designed it all first and set it in motion."

"You can't prove that scientifically. You have to rely on faith," Andrew said, thinking that was the end of the argument.

"So do you. Your beliefs require faith just as mine do."

"Not at all. I rely on science and reason."

"Science and reason cannot explain how the universe went from having no life to having life. There is a leap there that science cannot explain. So, how do you know it happened the way you think it happened? You just have to believe, right?"

"Not as much as you."

"Well, I'm okay with that. I don't mind the unknown."

Exhaustion was overcoming Andrew. Between his

injuries and the hermit's ridiculous ideas, he could hardly think anymore. He was disappointed that he had been forced to destroy the old man's arguments, but Michael was the one who pressed the issue, so he deserved it. Still, Andrew was determined to land a few more jabs.

"I had you all wrong," he said to the old hermit.

"In what way?"

"I didn't know you were a heartless conservative."

"Heartless?" Michael said with a surprised look. "Would a heartless person save your life? Would a heartless person take care of a total stranger in the wilderness? Would a heartless person feed you and take care of your wounds? Just because I may be conservative, as you have labeled me, doesn't mean I fit with your preconceived notion of conservatives. I don't ask for praise for doing what I think any human being would do, but I have a hard time understanding such ingratitude."

Michael stood up and walked to Andrew's chair. Andrew sensed that he had finally pushed the right buttons, but he was worried about what the old hermit might do to him. Bending down to Andrew, Michael picked him up and carried him to his tent. He placed Andrew gently on his mattress and turned to leave.

Just before reaching the tent door, Michael turned back to Andrew.

"There are more important things than scoring points in an argument. You speak of compassion and helping others, but you have shown little compassion for me. You claim to be compassionate and yet your way of trying to win an argument is to make personal attacks. There isn't much compassion there."

Michael turned to go, but was stopped by Andrew.

"You shouldn't have killed the wolf. He was my friend."

Michael looked at Andrew with a perplexed expression.

"He wasn't trying to kill me. It was a misunderstanding. He was confused. You should have just scared him away."

Michael walked away.

"I think you've spent too much time out here," Andrew yelled.

# Chapter 25: The End

Michael stayed with Andrew and took care of him until he could get around on his own. The two hadn't spoken much since their discussion by the fire. When Andrew was nearly at full strength, Michael came to him, shook his hand and said goodbye. Andrew never saw the old hermit again.

As summer drew to a close, Andrew felt discouraged. Despite his best efforts to help and save the valley and its animals, there was nothing more he could do. He had done everything he could and the valley was still in bad shape. Evan had done irreparable harm and Andrew now believed that Michael was partially responsible for neglecting the valley for so long and allowing it to get out of balance.

"I can't even imagine what shape it would be in if I hadn't come when I did," he thought.

Now that Gray Protector was dead, Andrew didn't feel like there was anything keeping him there. All of his friends were gone and there appeared to be very little food for animals to live on. Andrew wondered how it all had happened.

"Could I have done more? Is there something I missed?"

Andrew questioned himself, but he knew he had done more than what was reasonable. With his knowledge and capabilities, there wasn't really anything else that could be expected of him. He had accomplished what he had been sent to the valley to accomplish. He had provided the structures to promote fairness, but the animals had resisted it.

"Maybe it was Michael. Maybe the animals sensed him snooping around and they knew they couldn't trust him. It is clear that the only reason Gray Protector mistakenly attacked me is because he sensed Michael's unworthy presence."

Andrew thought of Michael and his naïve religious beliefs. He pitied the man for his delusions.

"The old hermit actually believes God is in charge of this valley."

Andrew knew this was a ridiculous notion. God was supposed to be wise and all-knowing. His followers alleged he was loving and compassionate, but Andrew knew better.

"If there were a God, how would he let something

like this happen to such a beautiful place? Why wouldn't he do something to help this place? Why wouldn't he save this valley? Why wouldn't he spare these animals, plants and trees?"

The answer to his question was obvious.

"There is no God and things like this prove it. A loving God would protect the valley and animals. A merciful God would not let deer get stuck in a river to drown. There is no God. There is me. I saved that deer. I helped the animals and I helped the plants. I gave this valley hope and yet it wasn't enough. I could only do so much. There was no God to save it, so I did my best. I tried to stop the bear from destroying everything but I am only one man. I cannot do it all. God doesn't love this valley because God doesn't exist. I exist."

Andrew was furious now. He wished his family could see the proof that God did not exist. He wished he could show them that if God did exist, he wasn't loving, kind or merciful. God was cruel, cold and not worthy of praise or adoration. God was false but this was real. His family lived in a bubble where they pretended that everything was fine and God provided all good things.

"They don't see God the destroyer. If they were confronted with *this*, they would conclude the same thing as I have: there is no God; there never was a God; there never will be a God."

He looked upon the valley he loved so much. He searched for some sign of life. He wanted the animals to watch him, but they were gone. With a backpack filled with provisions to last four days, Andrew hiked to the lower part of the valley. As he reached the edge of the valley, he noticed the midges and mosquitoes seemed to be less prevalent there.

He looked back at his domain and sighed. It was the last time he ever saw it. Turning his back, he was happy to see a beautiful doe up ahead and he followed her and the river downstream.

# Chapter 26: The Return

The adjustment to society was harsh. Andrew had been away for almost two years. He desperately hoped things might have paused while he was gone but they just went on as furiously as before. He felt as if he had been left behind.

He tried to reconnect with friends and, while they were thrilled to see him and become reacquainted, they had moved on to other friends and other candidates leaving little to no time for him.

His new life was difficult. He felt like he had no purpose; nothing to get him excited. The news he saw was depressing. The President had followed through on all his promises and, while unemployment was down and the economy was growing, all of the programs and progress Andrew had worked hard for over the years were severely damaged or outright disbanded.

Corporations seemed to be controlling the market as the government's role had been reduced. Drilling operations had expanded, border security had been tightened, radical Muslims were being labeled as "terrorists", social programs had been slashed and the rich were enjoying lower tax rates. This all made Andrew sick, but there was nothing he could do about it. He felt powerless.

After spending three weeks back in society, Andrew decided his place really was in the wilderness. Things made sense to him there and he knew what his role was. All of the animals looked to him as provider and protector.

"How are they doing without me?" He often wondered.

One evening, he went to a park to meditate. The park was empty except for a robin eating some crumbs next to the bench on which he was sitting. He thought of Rob as he watched it hop around for a few minutes. He wondered how Rob was doing.

"How can I just abandon him like that? He's probably looking for me. He needs me. They all need me. I have to go back."

Andrew realized he had come back to society to figure out where his heart really was. He needed to see the mess of society to realize how good he had it in the valley. It was all part of the universe's plan to get him to continue to improve the valley and make it into the utopia he had envisioned.

He knew the deer would come back to the valley once they saw he was staying for good. He could plant some more trees, water them and make sure they got enough sunlight. The squirrels would regroup and roam the valley once more. Andrew knew he could organize a system where they would all have equal opportunity and justice. He even thought of planting a garden so he could grow food and ration it for the animals.

"I didn't get enough time to help the valley adjust to Evan's absence. It was Evan's fault that things got out of whack; I just inherited his mess. Things are as they should be now. I can elevate the valley to where it should be. I will help integrate the wolves so the animals won't be afraid of them. I will not give up until everything is fair."

Andrew felt his heart stir. The helplessness he felt vanished as he thought of all the good he could continue to do in the valley.

"I'm going back!" He determined as he stood up.

He started walking back to his friend's house when he noticed someone else in the park. It was a woman carrying a stack of signs. She walked to one end of the park and planted a sign in the grass. The sign read "Brenda Smith for City Council".

The woman walked toward Andrew and planted a sign a few feet from where he was standing. She smiled at him and started to walk away.

"Are you Brenda?" He asked.

"Yes," the woman replied.

"How's the race going?"

"Not great. I am not making the impact I hoped I would. I'm facing some tough opposition."

"What do you think about the tax rates these days?"

"Way too low! The corporations are getting a windfall and the people in this country are paying for it with *their* money. It's ridiculous. This country is being destroyed. Corporations have all the wealth while they are making things harder on the lower class and destroying the environment and the salmon population."

"My name is Andrew. I'm a liberal." He said.

"I'm Brenda. I'm a liberal."

"I used to run national senatorial campaigns. I have worked on campaigns of all sizes. Do you need some help?"

"Yes, I do. As long as you can help me beat some conservative wack-jobs."

"Absolutely!" Andrew replied. "What do you know about this guy? What is his character? Does he have kids? Are they on drugs? Are there any scandals? If he's a conservative, there are plenty of labels we can attach to him to help voters realize who he really is."

"You're right," Brenda responded excitedly. "Well, his wife is a stay-at-home mother, so he's probably sexist. He supports traditional marriage so he's a bigot and a homophobe. And he was an executive for a manufacturing plant so he doesn't care about the environment and he's greedy."

"Perfect!"

"Do you have a debate coming up?"

"It's in two weeks."

"That's plenty of time to prepare. Let's go to a café and start planning."

As he talked with Brenda about how to embarrass and defeat her opponent, Andrew realized that this was where he was really needed. He needed to push forward his agenda so he could help people and the environment. In fact, by rejoining the world of politics, he could still save the valley through legislation.

"I can serve and help *everyone* this way."

Andrew's mind raced through the candidates in the big national races. He thought there were a few of them who could use his expertise. Once he gave Brenda some free advice, he would begin the process of finding the right campaign job.

It would not be easy; it would not happen overnight, but Andrew knew that he could turn things around in the country, just like he had in the valley. The universe had another job for him and he would put his whole heart and soul into making society better.

# Afterward

*Winter came and covered the valley in snow. Andrew's camp was completely buried, along with all of his bins and coolers. An avalanche in early spring wiped everything away. There was no sign of Andrew left behind.*

*Years passed and the valley slowly returned to its previous state. Each spring brought new beginnings. Animals flocked to the valley as trees blossomed and sunlight melted away the last bits of snow. Birds chirped in the treetops and deer grazed near the lake. A bear wandered toward some berry bushes. A wolf stood on top of a ridge and, seeing the bear in its territory, turned and scampered away to another valley.*

*Rob soared above the trees with a stomach full of worms. She swooped below the treetops where she found her four babies impatiently waiting for breakfast. She fed each one in turn, and then flew off to find more.*

*The valley, once again, thrived.*

THE END

# Index

"In satire, as in lapidary inscriptions, a man is not upon oath." (J. M. Treadwell) Though *Liberal In Nature* is a satire, and thus not meant to be critiqued for factual accuracy per se, there are some interesting scientific tidbits dealing with nature and its balances, which I drew from when writing *Liberal In Nature*.

This is not meant to be an exhaustive list of facts, nor is it meant to be hardcore zoological resource. It is aimed at providing some of the facts and ideas behind incidents and analogies in the novel.

If you have additional questions relating to the science in *Liberal In Nature*, please submit them to: info@liberalinnature.com

Frequently Asked Questions (Warning: SPOILERS!)

- Can apples grow in the wild?
- What do deer eat?
- What would happen to deer if you provided all their food for them?
- Why would the tall tree fall down after having some branches cut off?
- Are bears really bullies?
- Are wolves dangerous to animals and/or humans?
- Why do bucks duel?
- What would happen if the bucks were never able to duel?
- Are there any long-term consequences to removing obstacles for salmon to spawn?
- Could you really tell if a squirrel were pregnant?
- What would happen if too many salmon were able to spawn?
- Why would de-icing the trees in winter cause them to die?
- Would cutting off a bear's claws wake it from hibernation?
- What would happen to a bear with clipped claws?
- What do bears eat?
- What do wolves eat?
- Why would the temperature be warmer as one ascends a nearby hill?
- Why would insects start hatching in greater numbers?
- Are there really hermits living in the wilderness?
- Can someone really survive in the wilderness for 30

years?
- Why would the animals flee the valley?

## ANSWERS

### Can apples grow in the wild?

"In the wild, apples grow quite readily from seeds. However, like most perennial fruits, apples are ordinarily propagated asexually by grafting." (http://en.wikipedia.org/wiki/Apple) While it may be difficult for apples to grow spontaneously in the wilderness, it is possible that someone could plant an apple orchard in the wilderness that could survive, even under harsh winter conditions. But who would plant an apple orchard in the wilderness other than, perhaps, a crazy hermit?

### What do deer eat?

It depends on the type of deer, but they generally feed on: grasses, clovers, evergreen plants, acorns, fruits, nuts, aquatic plants and woody plants. (http://www.wildernessclassroom.com/www/schoolhouse/boreal_library/animals/deer.htm)

### What would happen to deer if you provided all their food for them?

Feeding any wild animal can cause the animal to become dependent on your food source, which can alter their behavior, their health and their ability to obtain food by natural means. If you start feeding a wild deer, you may have to continue it indefinitely for their protection. They can become domesticated and lose their natural, wild instincts making them vulnerable to predators. Feeding areas also can attract predators like coyotes and wolves. (http://www.anr.state.vt.us/site/html/reflect/jan11.htm)

**Why would the tall tree fall down after having some branches cut off?**

Trimming branches of any tree must be done cautiously and wisely. For instance, "Cedars typically have no more than a foot of new green growth. Branches pruned behind this green needle growth will not re-leaf. So, overzealous pruning can definitely harm cedar trees." (http://www.ehow.com/info_7954717_limbing-cedar-tree-hurt.html) One should trim sparingly and make sure that the trimming is balanced. If you trim branches from one side, the tree may become weighted to one side making it vulnerable to lean and eventually fall.

**Are bears really bullies?**

Depends on how you define "bully". Bears require a lot of space to live comfortably. They roam freely in order to find food, water and shelter. They are not overly aggressive animals, especially when it comes to humans. So, while they are big and strong and demand respect, it's probably not accurate to call them bullies. (http://www.bear.org/website/index.php?option=com_content&view=article&id=119:how-dangerous-are-black-bears&catid=17&Itemid=39)

**Are wolves dangerous to animals and/or humans?**

Wolves are most definitely dangerous to their prey - deer, elk, moose, mice, birds, fish, etc. (http://www.wolfweb.com/diet.html) Wolves, like bears, can be dangerous to humans if they feel threatened or something sets them off. In that case, wolves can do extreme damage to humans, including death. Those cases are rare, but not out of question. (http://www.conservationnw.org/pressroom/press-clips/wolves-and-humans-what-the-experts-say)

**Why do bucks duel?**

"Some buck fighting takes place all year round. A dominance order begins to become established immediately after birth. As six-month old fawns mature, a pecking order starts to take shape. Most of the fighting, if there is any fighting at this time, involves a flailing of hooves or aggressive posturing initially until the bucks get their first sets of antlers. Once the bucks' antlers are hardened, fighting can occur in the more traditional manner with which we're familiar." (http://www.nighthawkpublications.com/hunting/science-ch8.htm)

## What would happen if the bucks were never able to duel?

There may not be an answer to this question because it isn't usually an issue in nature. However, one could assume that if fighting were disallowed between bucks, no pecking order would be established, non-dominate bucks may be able to mate with does and it could weaken the herd. There is really no definite answer here.

## Are there any consequences to making it easy for salmon to spawn?

It is unclear what impact this would have, but as nature is set up for "survival of the fittest", having obstacles to spawning ensures that only the strong are able to survive and further populate the species. If the weaker salmon who would not otherwise make it to spawning beds are able to spawn through some intervention, this may introduce weakness in the species.

"Natural selection ensures the success of a species by favoring reproduction among animals which are adapted harmoniously with their environment, and by eliminating those not so well adapted...Maintaining that variety of gene-based traits is critical for survival."
(http://www.coastrange.org/salmon&survivalpg2.html)

## Could you really tell if a squirrel were pregnant?

A pregnant squirrel will be fatter than regular squirrels and will likely gather more nuts in the fall to prepare for the extra nourishment she will need to support her fetuses during winter. "Squirrels remain active all winter, but they tend to stay in their dens during cold or stormy weather. They are territorial only during reproduction, when pregnant or nursing females will drive off other squirrels that intrude on the nesting or den tree."
(http://www.wisconsinhunter.com/Pages/squirrels.html)

## What would happen if too many salmon were able to spawn?

Though it's debatable what the affects of over-spawning (or over-escapement) would be, it is possible that productivity could decrease due to competition between spawners, an overabundance of fry and parr could deplete their habitat of food to the point of collapse and it could result in waste. There are systems in place to regulate the salmon population, though some may be economically driven. (http://www.salmonguy.org/?p=646)

**Would de-icing the trees in winter cause them to die?**

Ice can provide protective insulation to some trees. Though weight of ice on branches can cause damage, removing ice altogether can expose the branches and trunk to harsh winter conditions. So, while it may seem counterintuitive, some people actually spray water on their trees to get that protective coat of ice. (http://www.gardenguides.com/96653-protect-lemon-tree-winter.html)

**Would cutting off a bear's claws wake it from hibernation?**

Let's not test this one. Though hibernation does slow a bear's heart-rate, it is actually not unconscious so some activity within a bear's cave could bring it out of hibernation. (http://www.bear.org/website/bear-pages/black-bear/hibernation/190-do-black-bears-hibernate.html)

**What would happen to a bear with no claws?**

Not sure on this one either. Bears use their claws for digging, climbing, clawing trees to mark territory, tearing and catching prey, etc. Having no claws would inconvenience the bear and slow it down to some degree, but it would likely be able to manage okay. (http://en.wikipedia.org/wiki/Bear)

**What do bears eat?**

Bears eat berries, insects, fish, small game, honey, carcasses of killed animals and whatever other food source that becomes available. (http://en.wikipedia.org/wiki/Bear)

**What do wolves eat?**

"Wolves are carnivores (meat eaters) but they will eat other foods as well. Their diet ranges from big game, such as elk and moose, to earthworms, berries and grasshoppers.

To avoid using too much energy catching their food, wolves prey on weaker members of a herd, such as old, young or sick animals. In summer, when the herds migrate, wolves eat mice, birds and even fish. They may also eat carrion." (http://www.wolfweb.com/diet.html)

## Why would the temperature be warmer as one ascends a nearby hill?

Within a valley, the area just above the valley floor and below the higher part of the valley is called the thermal belt, or thermal zone. This area can be anywhere from five to ten degrees warmer than above or below it as warmer air is trapped between areas of colder air. (http://polk.ces.ncsu.edu/content/TheThermalBelt&source=polk) and (http://apollo.lsc.vsc.edu/classes/met130/notes/chapter3/drainage3.html)

## Why would insects start hatching in great numbers?

Insects, such as midges, are a common food for fish. If the number of fish decreases, then more insects will hatch.

## Are there really hermits living in the wilderness?

Yes! (http://www.hermitary.com/articles/american.html)

and
(http://blogfromahermit.com/2008/10/24/documenting-a-life-hermit-dick-proenneke-alone-in-the-wilderness/)

## Can someone really survive in the wilderness for 30 years?

Why not? If you have the skills and knowledge, you can live off the land like many of our ancestors.

## Why would the animals flee the valley?

Animals go where the food is. Once a food source is depleted, the animals will migrate elsewhere. In addition, if a predator moves into a particular area, the other animals may move out.

Made in the USA
Lexington, KY
03 December 2011